GRAVEDIGGER

A RINEHART SUSPENSE NOVEL

A RINEHART SUSPENSE NOVEL

A Dave Brandstetter Mystery

GRAVEDIGGER

Joseph Hansen

HOLT, RINEHART AND WINSTON
New York

Copyright © 1982 by Joseph Hansen

Published by Holt, Rinehart and Winston,
383 Madison Avenue, New York, New York 10017.

Published simultaneously in Canada by Holt, Rinehart
and Winston of Canada, Limited.

Library of Congress Cataloging in Publication Data

Hansen, Joseph, 1923-
Gravedigger.
(A Rinehart suspense novel)
I. Title.
PS3558.A513G7   813'.54   81-6381   AACR2
ISBN: 0-03-056063-2

FIRST EDITION

Designer: *Lucy Castelluccio*

Printed in the United States of America
10 9 8 7 6 5 4 3 2 1

ISBN 0-03-056063-2

For Bill Harding

GRAVEDIGGER

A RINEHART SUSPENSE NOVEL

1

When last he had noticed, nothing was out here but bare hills above an empty beach. He was jolted by how much time must have passed—not years but decades. Now expensive ranch houses of distressed brick sprawled under low shake roofs on wide lots back of white rail fences. Trees had grown tall, mostly lacy eucalyptus, but even an occasional wind-bent cypress. The streets curved with the curves of the hills. Sometimes he glimpsed the blue water of backyard swimming pools where no one swam because the wind off the sea was cold though the sun shone in a clear blue sky.

He got lost among the empty suburban morning streets but at last he found Sandpiper Lane and a mailbox with the number 171, and parked the Triumph by a little palm whose hairy fans rattled in the wind. He climbed out of the car and the wind blew in his ears. When it stopped for breath, he could hear the distant surf. He heard no nearby sounds, human sounds. Even if you lived out here, you had to go to work, to school. If a wife kept at home by young children sat drinking coffee and watching television in a kitchen, her windows were closed, the sound didn't reach the street.

The mailbox at 171 needed a new coat of black paint. Rust showed at the welds. Leaves and litter strewed the driveway that was a half-circle. They crunched under his soles. He stepped over newspapers, thick, held folded by loops of grubby cotton string, print faded by sunlight, paper turning color from the weather. SEARCH FIVE STATES FOR MASS MURDERER a headline read. AZRAEL REPORTED IN MEXICO, CANADA read another. He peered through small panes of dusty glass in garage doors. No cars were parked inside.

A dozen dry shades of red and brown, eucalyptus leaves lay heaped at the foot of the front door. The door was recessed, its yellow enamel cracked and, near the bottom, peeling, curling back on itself. The door must have looked cheerful once. It looked sad now. Dave pushed a bell button. Chimes went off inside the house. He waited but no one came. He rang the chimes again, inhaling the dark insistent eucalyptus smell. He rubbed his nose. He used a tarnished brass knocker at eye level in the middle of the door. Its rattle raised only echoes. Rubber squealed in the street. He turned. A new little red pickup truck swung in at the driveway of a house across the street. From the bed of the truck, a surfboard flashed signals at the sun.

The truck rocked to a halt in front of the door of the house and a boy jumped out of the cab and ran for the door. All of him but his face was covered by a black wetsuit, red and yellow stripes down arms and legs. He hopped on one foot while he jingled keys and tried to get one into the door. Dave ran down the driveway of 171,

2

holding up a hand, calling out to the boy to wait a minute. The boy flung a panicky look over his shoulder and disappeared into the house. The slam of the door was loud in the stillness of a moment's drop in the wind.

Dave trotted across the street, up the drive, dodged the little red truck, and rang another set of door chimes. He panted. He was getting old. Running wasn't natural to him anymore. From inside the house he heard a shout but couldn't make out the words. Were they "Go away!" or "Come in!"? He waited. The apple-green enamel on this door was fresh and dustless, as if it had been laid on yesterday. He regarded it for two or three minutes, whistling softly between his teeth. Then the door opened.

"Sorry," the boy said. He wore a red sweatshirt now and was tying the drawstring of a pair of red sweatpants. His hair was a blond mop. He was barefoot. "I had to get to the bathroom. You want them, across the street?"

"Westover," Dave said, "Charles. Any idea where he's gone? It looks as if it's been a while."

"What are you about?" the boy said. "All kinds of people keep coming. Once it was a marshal."

"I'm about insurance," Dave said. "Life insurance." He watched the boy start to shut the door and said, "No, I don't sell it. I investigate death claims." He took out his wallet and handed the boy a card. The boy read it and looked startled. "Brandstetter," he said, and smiled. "Hey, sure. I saw you on TV—Tom Snyder or somebody. You solve murders when the police can't do it."

"The police are busy," Dave said. "I'm not busy. How long has the Westover house been empty?"

"A week, ten days." He frowned. "Who's murdered?"

"Maybe no one," Dave said. "Maybe Serenity Westover."

"Oh, wow." Noon-blue sea light had been in the boy's eyes. It clouded over. He stared at Dave, at Dave's mouth, where the name had come from. He said numbly, "Serenity?"

"Do you know her?"

"We were in the same kindergarten, grade school, high school." The boy looked past Dave, maybe at the house across the street. "We had our first date together. Sixth grade." The wind blew cold, and that may have been what made him shiver. Or it may have been something else. "Jesus." He said it softly to himself, then backed inside and told Dave to come in. Dave stepped in and the boy shut the door. "I'm freezing," he said, and walked off. "You like some coffee? Some breakfast? I'm starved. I didn't eat before I left this morning. God, that water was cold." He was out of sight now, but Dave followed his voice. "There's a storm down off Baja, and the surf is way up, but you get so numb all you do is fall off. And after while, anyway, all you can think of is how badly you have to pee, and that's not easy in a wetsuit." Dave found him in a spacious kitchen of waxed wood cabinets and waxed red brick under sloping beams. "I should have gone to school. I knew how it would be. I've tried it before in weather like this. I don't learn very fast." A circle of flame burned high under a red-orange teakettle. The boy scooped coffee beans into a grinder of the same color. The grinder whirred and rattled while the boy held his hand on it. When the motor quit whining, he looked at Dave. "How do you mean, 'maybe'?"

"Her father claims she was one of the girls murdered at that ranch in the desert. The ones whose bodies they've been digging up. It's been in the news."

"Oh, wow," the boy said again. "What makes him think that?"

There was a breakfast bar with neat bentwood stools that had cushions of natural linen. Dave sat on one of the stools, took an envelope out of his jacket pocket, and slipped from the envelope a smaller envelope that was soiled, rumpled, and addressed in a childlike hand in blue ball-point ink. "You want to look at this for me?"

The boy came to the bar, carrying the clear plastic part of the coffee grinder that held the pulverized beans. He looked at the envelope without touching it. He looked at Dave. Stricken. With a finger, Dave pushed the envelope closer to him. He said:

"Is that her writing?"

The boy nodded. He gave a sad little smile. "It was always like that, never got any better. I've got a lot of her letters. I don't know why I keep them. She changed. She wasn't the same anymore. The way she was acting, I didn't want anything to do with her. She didn't want anything to do with me." He set down the container. The coffee smell that rose from it was dense and appetizing. He picked up the envelope and squinted at the blurry postmark. "Perez," he said, and stared at Dave again.

"Go ahead," Dave said, "open it. Take out what's inside." What was inside was a letter on dimestore writing paper in the same clumsy, childish hand, the same cheap ball point. Also a snapshot. The boy unfolded the letter and read aloud under his breath: "Dear Daddy. So you won't worry about me, I want you to know that I am very happy, now. I have found someplace where I can be at peace. . . ." He let the letter drop. He picked up the snapshot. "Oh, wow," he said again, and looked at Dave

5

with tears in his eyes. "She was there. Look. That's her, standing right next to Azrael. Smiling. Oh, wow."

"You're sure?" Dave said.

"I saw her every day of my life almost," he said, "from the time when we were babies. Of course I'm sure."

"There are six girls in the photo," Dave said. "You mean the dark, roundfaced one with the long straight hair?"

"That's Serenity." The kettle began rattling. The boy picked up the container of ground coffee and went back to the counter beside the burner deck. He dumped the ground coffee into a glass coffee maker, fitted its sections together, picked up the kettle by its handsome bentwood handle, poured the boiling water in, set the kettle down.

"There wasn't much of a lens in that camera," Dave said. "The image isn't sharp. And she's not so different from a hundred thousand other girls her age."

The boy switched off the burner. "It's her." He got coffee mugs down from a cupboard, brought them to the breakfast bar, set them there. He picked up the grubby envelope again and peered at the postmark. "This was mailed almost two years ago. Just after she ran away."

"And in two years," Dave said, "she could have run away from Azrael, too, couldn't she? That's what makes Banner Insurance nervous about this claim. They're going to be even more nervous when I report that the man who filed the claim has also run away. Why did Serenity run away—can you tell me?"

The boy winced at him. "Is this how you do your job? I mean—don't you know anything about the Westovers?"

"That there were four of them, Charles, Anna, Serenity, and Lyle—father, mother, two children. I know their ages and that they live, or lived, across the street here. I have a telephone number that no one answers. I can't find an office, so I assume Charles Westover used his home. He's an attorney."

"Used to be," the boy said. "He got disbarred for bribing witnesses and went to jail for a year. That was when Serenity took off."

"Disappointed in her father?" Dave said.

The boy laid strips of bacon in a frying pan. "She could never be that. It was her mother. Her mother divorced him and Serenity couldn't forgive her for that and they fought all the time and finally Serenity left." The boy opened a big coppertone refrigerator and put the bacon package back and brought out eggs. "No—she and her father were crazy about each other. This thing about bribing the witnesses and all that took about a year or something, and he was in deep trouble, you know? And he didn't have time for her or anybody. He was trying to save himself, I suppose." The boy broke eggs into a terra-cotta-color mixing bowl and put the shells down a disposal that gulped and shuddered. "We didn't see him. He used to be friendly with my folks, he and Anna. But when this happened, he kept away. My dad didn't judge him. He was a friend, all right? But Chass was ashamed I guess, or afraid or something, and we hardly saw him at all. I mean, he'd speak if you said hi when he was coming out of his driveway or something, but he wouldn't drop over like before and he stopped going to the beach club and anything like that. Just holed up over there. And his wife was the same."

"And Serenity?"

"She went crazy, sort of. I mean, we were buddies—like

brother and sister, if you want to put it like that. We played together all the time when we were little and it was just"— he was beating the eggs with a fork and he moved his shoulders in a shrug—"a companionship that went on, all right? I used to wonder if we were in love, sometimes. I could never answer that." Butter sizzled in a frying pan, and he poured in the beaten eggs and set the bowl in the sink and stirred the eggs around over the burner-deck flame with the fork. "It just seemed like we'd always been together and so, maybe, we always would be. But then this rotten thing happened that her father did and she stopped coming around. I tried for a while to get her to. I mean, it was very"—he reached down plates from a cupboard—"I missed her, I was sad, I was lonesome, okay? But she began running around with beach bums and druggies from Venice, a whole crowd of freaks. She seemed to want to do every crazy thing they were doing. Drunk half the time, wandering around spaced out on God knows which kind of pills the rest of the time. Once, her mother went and found her living with some greasy weirdo that called himself a poet, in a ratty old dump, one room with a mattress on the floor. She wouldn't leave for her mother, and her mother asked me to go along to try to get her to come home. She was passed out on reds, and I just picked her up and carried her out to the car." He spooned the eggs out of the pan onto the waiting plates. He turned off the burners. He forked bacon onto the plates. He brought the plates to the breakfast bar and set them down. He gave a little bleak laugh at himself. "Hell, I forgot forks, I forgot napkins." He got these from drawers. The forks were good Danish steel. The napkins were linen that matched the seatcovers

8

of the stools. He sat on the stool beside Dave, then got off it and went for coffee and sugar, spoons, and cream in a squat carton. He sat on the stool again. "Then the trial came and he went to jail."

"He didn't try to appeal?"

"No. Maybe he was tired of fighting. Maybe Anna saying she was through with him forever made him give up or something. That's what my father said. He's a psychiatrist." The boy began eating hungrily. "And that's when Serenity ran away." He cut at a bacon strip with the edge of his fork, stopped, looked at Dave. "You don't think he's right—Serenity wasn't one of those girls Azrael buried?"

"I don't know enough yet," Dave said, "to think anything. But for what it's worth, Banner Insurance is in doubt. Three of the recovered bodies have been identified and claimed. Three no one has come for. I guess they didn't send their parents letters and snapshots. One of them could have been Serenity. Blood type, hair color, height, and general skeletal conformation all match. But the girl in question was a perfect specimen—no dental work, never broke a bone."

"Serenity never broke a bone," the boy said. "Her teeth were perfect." The boy worked on the bacon and eggs for a minute. Then he said, "They take a baby footprint in the hospital when you're born."

"These bodies weren't in a condition to yield footprints or fingerprints," Dave said. "But I'm glad to know about Serenity's teeth and bones. That helps. Thank you. And to answer your question—yes, this is how I do my job. And now I do know something about the Westovers, don't I." He gave the boy a tight little smile. "I appreciate your help." He tasted the coffee. It was first-rate. "And I appreciate the breakfast."

"I don't know where Chass went," the boy said.

"What about his wife? Where is she now? Anna?"

"I think she runs a school for little kids, a playschool. Someplace in West L.A." He wrinked his forehead. "What does she call it? The Hobbit School. Yeah."

"Thanks. I'll look her up." Dave ate for a few minutes, drank some more coffee, lit a cigarette. "What about the son, what about Lyle? Does he go to college somewhere?"

"Juilliard in New York," the boy said. "Only not this year. He was around. I don't know, but I think he was working. Maybe to help his father out." The boy went away and came back with a brown pottery ashtray for Dave. He set it on the counter. "He's a musical genius." The boy got onto his stool again, sipped some coffee, laughed wryly. "All the kids thought he was a retard, a moron. He has this very bad speech defect, all right? And he wasn't any good at anything kids do—running, swimming, playing any kind of games. Very bad physical coordination, almost like a spastic, you know? And it turned out he's a musical genius. We treated him really badly, really mean. Nobody could stand him. He didn't do anything to deserve it. Kids are cruel, right?"

"But Lyle's not there now," Dave said. "And hasn't been there. Also for a week or ten days. Could he have gone away with his father?"

"I guess so. They never seemed to have anything to say to each other." The boy shook his head, frowning. "I don't see why he'd go. He had a lot of friends coming around all the time. Music coming out of the windows over there—sometimes till two in the morning."

10

"Did Serenity like him? Did he like her?"

"Not when we were really small," the boy said, "but when we all grew up a little, she got mad at us when we called him stupid and told him to get lost. Then, pretty soon, it wasn't a problem anymore. He got all wrapped up in music, practicing all day—only ten, eleven years old. Yes, sure, Serenity liked him—loved him, didn't she? Sure. I guess he loved her too. I never heard any different."

Dave checked his wristwatch, drank the last of the coffee from his mug, got off the stool. "I'd better find Anna Westover," he said. "You've got my card?" The boy nodded and got off his stool. Dave said, "If Westover or Lyle shows up over there, will you phone me? I'll be grateful. If I'm not there, leave your message on the tape, all right?" The boy said he would, and Dave looked around for the way out. The boy led him, opened the apple-green door. The sea wind crowded in. The sun hadn't warmed it. When Dave was halfway down the drive, the boy called:

"I wish it would be Serenity who shows up."

"So do I." Dave lifted a hand, walked on down the drive, crossed the street. He started to get into the Triumph and halted. He looked back. The green door was closed. He went to the 171 mailbox and opened it. It was jammed with envelopes. He shut the box, got into the Triumph, and drove away.

2

Anna Westover said, "Isn't it tiresome how right folk wisdom always turns out to be?" In an empty schoolroom strewn with naptime blankets, building blocks, toy xylophones, little red tables, little red chairs, she stood, small, thin, and brittle, facing a window where the clear morning light showed every line of worry and disappointment in her handsome face. She smiled wryly, and more lines appeared to frame her generous mouth. "'As ye sow, so shall ye reap.'" She sighed, looked at Dave, straightened her shoulders. "How much I would have done differently, if only I hadn't been so sure of myself."

Outside the window, under old pepper trees, little kids in bright sweaters toddled and hopped, chirping and squeaking in a yard of grass-cracked blacktop, among gaudily painted swings, seesaws, jungle gyms. "It looks like a cheerful life," Dave said. "There have to be worse ways to earn your living."

"I agree," she said. "It's the loneliness I feel sorry about. I might have had my father and mother again, but a choice was given me a long time ago, and I chose my husband. Now I don't have him and I don't have them."

"People who make either/or propositions to their children can't be much of a loss," Dave said.

She had fine, clear, gray eyes, and they searched his face now skeptically. "Have you children, Mr. Brandstetter?"

He shook his head. "I was one once. Does that help?"

"Almost not at all," she said. She crossed her arms on her breast, clutching her arms. She walked around the room on legs that were good and straight and must have been beautiful before they became too thin. "What you want for your children is that they never stumble and fall and hurt themselves. Suddenly emotions take charge of you that you never knew you possessed. It's appalling how strong they are. Common sense hasn't a chance." She stopped and looked at him again. "But you mustn't think it's their fault—my parents, I mean. Of course they would be happy to have me back in the circle of their love again."

"Then, if you're lonely—" he began.

"I am also stubborn and ashamed. When I wanted to marry Chass, my father said he was no good, and that he would bring me sorrow and disgrace. He said he didn't have any moral fiber. He acknowledged that he was brilliant. He admitted that he had charm, grace, good looks, all of which would take him far in the law. But he saw into Chass as I couldn't see, and knew that intelligence, charm, grace, good looks don't add up to a man."

"What about ambition?" Dave said. "That's an expensive house out there at the beach. It takes hard work to earn a house like that. And he's only forty-five."

"Oh, yes." She nodded and smiled sadly with a corner of her mouth. "Ambition. Yes, indeed. The really dangerous ingredient for a no-good. That was what my father trusted least in Chass. Oh, yes." She laughed grimly. "Ambition he

13

did have. I thought it was wonderful. It wasn't. It was a disease, a cancer."

A small oriental boy stumbled and fell in the yard. A mountainous black woman in a tent-size flowered smock swooped down, gathered him against her massive breasts, petted him, crooned to him. His cries from beyond the plate glass sounded like the reedy bleat of a squeeze toy.

"I was so in love with him, so proud of him, so sure of him. I begged my father to help him. He thought he could make me let Chass go by refusing. Instead, I quit school myself, went to work, and paid his way through law school. He came out at the top of his class. I was vain, and I rubbed my father's nose in it. Wrong, how wrong he'd been. Oh, was I vain and foolish." Laughing sourly at herself, she began gathering up the small blankets, folding them, stacking them on the lower shelves of bookcases full of rubber balls, dolls, mallets, teddy bears. "And fond and foolish was my father. I thought, and perhaps he thought so too, that he was acting on the strength of evidence. He was a lawyer, after all. He took Chass into his firm, made him a junior partner. But it wasn't the strength of the evidence, was it? It was guilt at having let me sacrifice my own education, my future—'sacrifice' would have been the word he used to himself—to put Chass through law school instead of helping him, as he could so easily have done, so easily. Guilt. And chagrin at having misjudged the man his daughter loved."

"He wasn't with your father's firm," Dave said, "when this witness-bribing thing happened?"

"Oh, no." She began picking up the scattered small chairs and arranging them neatly at the tables. "Chass

14

didn't stay more than a few years. He chafed. Things moved too slowly. Then the chance to handle a big criminal case came his way. He begged my father to let him handle it under the firm's umbrella. But it wasn't that kind of firm. It was corporate law, civil law, property management, that tame sort of thing. My father distrusted criminal law. He wouldn't hear of it. And Chass left the firm." She opened a door, switched on a light in a washroom, came back with a sponge and, crouching, began to wipe off the tabletops. A faint smell of orange juice reached Dave. "He did well on his own. I didn't much like the clients he sometimes brought to dinner. I didn't like them in the same house with my children. But that didn't often happen." She gave a little dry chuckle. "Just too often. But"—she sighed, rose, moved to the next table, crouched again, wiped again—"he was happy. Things were moving fast. He liked the courtroom, the confrontations, the reality—that was what he called it—the reality of it all. And, of course, he loved winning. And he always seemed to win."

"And the money?" Dave said.

"And the money." She wiped another table, rose and took the sponge into the washroom. Dave heard water splash. Over the sound of the water, she called, "That was when we bought that pretentious house, where the damned wind never stops blowing. Serenity was six."

"And Lyle?" Dave wondered.

She came out with the sponge. "Five. And a great worry. He couldn't speak, he could only make funny noises. It turned out that was his way of speaking. It still is."

"Did you take him to therapists?"

She was wiping tabletops again. "Oh, yes. I believe sev-

15

eral of them went into other professions after encountering Lyle. At first, they insisted something was the matter with his brain." She found a spill spot on the asphalt tile floor and wiped the shiny surface clean. "He has the brain of an Einstein." She didn't sound pleased about Lyle. "If he wanted to speak, he'd speak. He simply can't be bothered."

"I'm told he's a fine musician," Dave said. "He was living with his father. Why was that?"

"It was his choice," she said briskly. "Ask him."

"Tell me where to find him and I will," Dave said.

"At Juilliard, in New York," she said.

"Not this winter," Dave said. "You mean you haven't seen him since he came home?"

"Is he home? I thought you said you couldn't find him."

"The boy across the street says he's been home, playing music at night, working during the day, to help his father out. The house is in poor shape. What happened to all that wonderful money? Did it go for his defense?"

"And he can't earn any more," she said. She stood in the washroom doorway, and smoked a cigarette. The motions she made were nervous. "He's disbarred. You knew that." She blinked. "The boy across the street? You mean little Scotty Dekker?" She laughed bleakly and shook her head. "How we misjudge children. I'd never have believed Scotty could understand a thing he saw or heard. A pretty little animal—that's what I always thought about Scotty."

"He's still pretty," Dave said, "and he's got eyes and ears, and maybe even a normal brain. But he evidently wasn't any closer to Lyle than you are. And he doesn't know where he's gone or why. Or his father, either. Where would they go, Mrs. Westover?"

"I don't know. And I don't know why it's so pressing.

16

What do you care? I suppose Chass finally ran from all the people he owes money to. The house is heavily mortgaged, for one thing. I presume he owes you money?"

"He doesn't," Dave said. "Do you hear from Serenity?"

Anna Westover stared. "Has something happened to her?"

"Do you know where she's been these past two years?"

"No. She never wrote, never telephoned. No."

"She wrote," Dave said, "to her father."

Anna Westover turned, threw away her cigarette. Dave heard the toilet flush. She came out of the washroom, came straight to him. "You have a way with you," she said, "like a good priest's, a father confessor's. But you aren't a father confessor, are you? You're something very different."

"Did your husband, ex-husband, come to you, or phone you for money at any time recently?"

"He would know better," she said. "After he got out of prison, he came once. But not for money. He wanted me to make love to him. I suppose he thought he could charm me back again, I don't know. He seemed very sad and shabby. I felt sorry for him, but I didn't let him do as he wanted. What is this about Serenity?"

Dave told her, showed her the letter, the snapshot.

"Dear God," she said, and sat down on one of the little round tables. "That swine. That son of a bitch." She was looking away. The window light was on her face again. Her face was taut. She turned it, lifted it to Dave. "You don't believe it, I hope. Because it isn't true, you know. It's simply a way for him to raise money. He saw the story about those poor, tragic girls on television, and he remembered he had that letter from Serenity, that photo. Oh, I know so well how his warped mind works. I can see him digging out

17

that insurance policy, rubbing his hands, sitting down at his desk to write that letter."

"Banner Insurance agrees with you," Dave said. "But how can you be sure? You say you haven't heard from her. The photo shows she was there. That is Serenity, isn't it? Scotty Dekker says it is."

"Why would she go there?" It was a cry of protest.

"She was on dope," Dave said. "She went some pretty low places, even before she ran away. Scotty told me about the room with the mattress and the rats in Venice."

"That was playacting," Anna Westover scoffed. "For my benefit. I was divorcing her cherished father. She was punishing me, trying to drive me back to him."

"And you weren't having any," Dave said.

"I knew him," she cried. "Serenity didn't. It wasn't reasonable. I'd forgiven him everything. There was a case where he won, and he was wild with elation—and the next day, the very next day, both principal witnesses were killed. Oh, certainly, by accident. Yes, of course. One drove off a cliff, the other set fire to his bed with a cigarette and immolated himself. I knew those weren't accidents. So did the district attorney. Those witnesses had been bought, hadn't they? And then killed to keep them from blackmailing Chass or his client later. They were not nice men."

"The district attorney couldn't make a case?"

"Not then," she said bitterly, "but he remembered and he waited and he made a case at last. Chass bought one too many witnesses for those gangsters who paid him so well. I knew. But what did Serenity know? How could I tell her?"

"You like folk wisdom," Dave said. "How about, 'The truth never hurt anybody'?"

"You never had children," she said angrily. "She was

18

fifteen years old. You can't reason with them at that age. The truth is the last thing they want to hear. He could do no wrong—don't you understand? So if I was divorcing him when he was in the deepest trouble of his life, who was wrong? Chass?" Her laugh despaired. "Forget it." She stood up. "And now you tell me she ran to that monster Azrael and he cut the living heart out of her and dumped her in a dirty hole in the desert. And that's my fault, too, isn't it?" She doubled her fists. "Oh, you are a horrible man. Get out. Get out of here."

"Just the messenger," Dave said. "I don't know that she is dead. No one knows. Why jump to conclusions?"

"Because that's she!" Anna Westover cried. "That's Serenity. Standing right next to him in that snapshot. That is my little girl, mister." And suddenly she was weeping. Hard and loud. She covered her face with her hands and ran stumbling into the washroom. She slammed the door and went on sobbing behind it. He went to the door and rapped gently. She quieted. He said:

"Don't cry. You could be right. He tried fraud, and when he didn't get the check, he figured someone like me would be coming around for the facts, and there weren't any facts, and anyhow what good was twenty-five thousand dollars going to do him? It wasn't enough to go to jail for. And that's why he disappeared. Where would he go, Mrs. Westover? Friends? His parents?"

"The only friends he had were vicious. He'd saved their rotten skins for them, but when he got into trouble, did any of them come to help him? Be serious." She opened the door, wiping her nose with tissues, wiping her reddened eyes. "He had no parents." Her laugh was brief and rueful. "That was part of his charm for me, wasn't it? An orphan.

The pathos of it." She touched Dave. "Find Serenity, Mr. Brandstetter." Her hand trembled against his chest. "He doesn't matter. Find her. Find her alive."

"Nothing would please me more," Dave said, "but I have to find her father too. It's my job. Where is he?"

"I don't know," she wailed. "How many times must I tell you that? Don't know, don't care. I'm nothing to him anymore, nothing to Lyle. They're nothing to me."

He didn't believe her. He changed the subject. He said, "Was there a woman?"

Her mouth opened in surprise. Then she laughed. Bleakly. "Sorry. He lied and cheated. But not that way."

"Sometimes the wife is the last to know."

"I'm not going to tell you how I know," she said, "but I do know—believe me."

"Right. Thank you." Dave crossed the shiny floor. When he reached for the doorknob, she caught up to him and gripped his arm. "Find Serenity," she begged again. "I don't want her to be one of those girls. That letter is old. She wouldn't stay with that monster. Why would she?"

"You tell me," Dave said.

"Don't believe Scotty." She shook her head, frantically. Tears were in her eyes again. "She wasn't bad. She just couldn't handle the breakup between Chass and me. That's all. She's a good child. Cheerful and bright."

"Try not to worry." Gently Dave pried her fingers from his sleeve. "He was betting on a long shot. There hasn't been a payoff. I don't think there ever will be. You keep remembering that."

And he stepped out into the cold noon sunshine.

3

"So he's missing," Salazar said. He dealt with homicides for the L.A. county sheriff's office. Dark-haired, honey-color, handsome, he looked sick today, sallow. His steel desk was heaped with files and photographs and forms. The photographs had ugly subjects, what Dave could see of them. "Does his family want him back?"

"Nobody's worried about him but me," Dave said.

"Signs of foul play?" Salazar drank coffee that steamed in a styrofoam cup. It burned his beautiful mouth. He breathed a little puff of steam. "Jesus," he said, and pawed for a cigarette pack among the papers. It was empty and he crumpled it. Dave held out his pack and, when Salazar took a cigarette, lit it for him with a slim steel lighter. He lit a cigarette for himself. Salazar turned in his chair to look out at the cold blue sky. "You have any real reason to think he's dead inside the house?"

"He expected money," Dave said. "Go look and see."

"His car there?" Salazar tried the coffee again, cautiously this time, eyeing Dave over the rim. "Did you check the garage?"

"It's empty," Dave said. "The mailbox is full."

Down the hall a man began to curse in Spanish.

"So he went someplace," Salazar said, "and didn't come back." Salazar's office was one of a row of cubicles that looked through plate glass at a broad room where fluorescent light fell cold on desks where telephones kept ringing, and at some of which men typed, or leaned back in chairs, talking to other men who stood holding papers. Or the men at the desks talked into the insistent phones. They frowned and made notes on pads with pencils or ball-point pens. Now Salazar looked past Dave out into that room. A scuffle was going on out there. The Spanish curses were louder now, and there were shouts from the English-speakers. Furniture slammed. There was a crash. Dave turned to look. Far off across the big room, where everyone was now standing up to watch, two men in neat jackets and short haircuts were struggling with a fat, brown-skinned boy whose hair was long and held by a rolled bandanna. They all three fell to the floor and were hidden from view by desks. Some of the men from the desks headed for the fight. Salazar said to Dave, "I could check to see if he's turned up dead after an accident. What kind of car was it, do you know?" He reached for his telephone.

Dave shook his head. "Have you got a phone book that covers that area?" Salazar had the book. Stacked with others on the floor. He crouched for it, slipped it out of the stack, wiped dust off its slumped spine with his hand, laid it in front of Dave. Dave studied him. He was sweating and breathing hard. "You're sick," he said. "Should you even be here?"

Salazar sat down, making a face of disgust. "Fucking

flu," he said. "Had it since Christmas. Makes you weak. I'm all right." He wiped the film of sweat off his face with tissues from a torn, flower-patterned box almost empty. He nodded at the directory. "You going to call somebody?"

Dave flopped open the book. In the big outer room, the fat brown boy stopped cursing in Spanish and began snarling like an animal. Metal furniture crashed again. Dave turned to look. A file cabinet lay on its side, spewing paper. Six men loaded the brown boy out of the room like a captive beast. Dave blinked at Salazar.

"PCP," Salazar said. "It takes them that way."

Dave located the name Dekker and found a Dekker paired with Sandpiper Lane in a gray column on a gray page. He punched for an outside line. He punched the Dekker number. Scotty had not gone to school. He told Dave what Dave asked to know, Dave thanked him, hung up, and passed the phone to Salazar. "It's a Rolls, late sixties, a four-door hardtop, two-tone, brown and gold. Westover is five ten, hazel eyes, brown hair beginning to thin on top at the back, no extra weight on him, maybe one-forty. Lately, he didn't always remember to shave."

Salazar held the receiver to his ear. He punched the phone buttons with the rubber end of a yellow pencil. He asked Dave, "Marks or scars?"

"The tip of one ear is missing. The informant doesn't remember which ear. He's just a neighbor kid."

Salazar relayed Westover's description to someone in an office who had to do with keeping track of unidentified corpses. None of the unidentified corpses on hand fitted the description. Salazar tried another number and told someone about the Rolls. He waited a long time, receiver trapped at his ear by his shoulder, drank coffee, finished his cigarette, snubbed out the cigarette in a square glass ashtray heaped with short, yellow-stained butts. He said "Yes" into the receiver, listened some more, grunted "Thanks" and replaced the receiver. "No abandoned or smashed-up Rollses, either," he said.

"Because it isn't in the garage," Dave said, "doesn't have to mean Westover drove it away. A car like that? Why didn't somebody steal it? The garage is padlocked, but that doesn't signify. He could be in the house tied up and gagged. He could be in there murdered. It's an expensive house in an expensive neighborhood. Why didn't somebody break in, kill him, plunder the place, and steal the car?"

"Because that's not the obvious explanation," Salazar said. "The obvious explanation is that the man has huge debts he can't pay. He was grabbing at straws, trying to defraud your insurance company. When it didn't pay off right away, he packed up and cleared out."

"His son disappeared at the same time," Dave said. "Eighteen, nineteen. Name of Lyle. Music student."

"What are you saying now?" Salazar asked. "That the son killed him and drove off with the family car?"

"Off the record," Dave said, "no. But if I said yes for the record, would you send a team out there?"

"Look at this mess." Salazar picked up and dropped the loose stack of files, papers, photographs, on his desk. One of the photographs slid to the floor on Dave's side. He bent and picked it up. A middle-aged black in a Hawaiian shirt lay in a leakage of blood by a back-alley trash module. Dave laid the photo on the desk. The black's bulging eyes stared at him. He looked as if the last thing he could imagine was being dead. Salazar said, "We had one thousand five hundred and thirty-two homicides in this county in the last eight months." He tried to straighten the papers. "You haven't even got a crime. Why won't Westover be back tomorrow? Why won't the kid? Have you got another cigarette?"

Dave gave him another cigarette.

Romano's was crowded for lunch. It was dark after the sunglare of the street, and inside the door he blundered against backs and elbows. The bar at the front was small, couldn't hold a lot of patrons, and latecomers waiting for tables had to stand out here by the reservation desk with their drinks, if they'd been so lucky as to get drinks. Narrowing his eyes, trying to adjust them to the lack of light, Dave looked for Mel Fleischer. Mel was late too. Dave excused himself and edged between the drinkers, hoping Amanda had got here on time. Max Romano would have held the corner table for Dave forever, but Dave had finally talked him out of that. Dave's showing up was too often chancy. It wasn't fair to the hungry, it wasn't fair to Max. Today, everything was all right because Amanda was there, in a nubby natural-wool thing, bright blue scarf knotted at her throat, a puffed-up mockery of a 1920s boy's cap, oatmeal-color, tilted on her neat little skull. She had a tall margarita for herself and a smile for him. A young man sat with her—a stranger to Dave. Amanda seemed pleased with him.

She said, "Dave Brandstetter, Miles Edwards."

Edwards rose and was tall. He shook Dave's hand firmly,

smiled with handsome teeth, claimed it was nice to meet Dave, and sat down again. He wore a suit that looked expensive without making an issue of it. His dark hair and trim black beard and mustache, his long, dense, dark childlike lashes, contrasted with the pale gray of his eyes. He was tanned, except where dark glasses had kept the sun from his skin.

Amanda studied Dave. "You look tired and not happy."

The chairs were barrel-type in crushed black velvet. Dave sank into his with a sigh. "This case is not a case like any case I ever had before, and nobody is helping me—almost nobody."

"Take heart." Amanda offered him a cigarette, one of the long, slim, brown kind. "Remember the Little Red Hen." She lit the cigarette for him, then sat straight and waved into the candle shadows. "Glenlivet, please, a double, on the rocks?"

"And that car," Dave said. "You and I should never shop together. My tendency to impulse buying is bad enough without you backing me up. That car is a bone-cracker."

"What kind of car?" Edwards said.

"TR," Dave said. "It had to be small to get into my driveway." To Amanda: "Does he know about my driveway?"

"There's no way to describe it," she said. "Where have you been—a long way?"

"Up the coast beyond Zuma," Dave said, "back to a nursery school in West L.A., downtown to the sheriff's. Then out the freeway to Hollywood, and you. It's like riding in a dice cup."

"What car should we have gotten?" she said.

"That big brown Jaguar."

"But the driveway," she said.

"I'll hire a bulldozer. I'll change the driveway."

"Also you wanted to save gas," she said.

"Now I want to save me," he said. Max Romano himself, plump, his few remaining black curls plastered across his bald dome, brought the Glenlivet, squat glass, much whiskey, little ice, the way Dave liked it. "Thanks, Max."

"You look pale." Max handed menus to Amanda and Edwards. Dave waved his away. Max frowned. "Are you sick?"

"Not hungry," Dave said. Usually he liked the thick garlic-and-cheese smells of Romano's, but this noon, they made him feel a little queasy. "I'm all right, Max. Just bad-tempered. I got up too early. Ruins the whole day."

"Something light on the stomach," Max suggested. "A fluffy little omelet"—he wiggled fat fingers to indicate delicacy—"with mozzarella?"

Dave winced. "Maybe. Later. We'll see." Max went off shaking his head, face puckered with worry. Dave told Edwards, "One person you never miss around Max is your mother."

"You never had one," Amanda said.

"I had nine," Dave said, "in rapid succession. But you're the nicest."

"Known Max a long time?" Edwards said.

"Since before you were born," Dave said. He took in some whiskey and lit another of Amanda's cigarettes. "And while I was sitting here boozing with dead friends and lovers, what were you doing with those thirty-four years?"

27

Edwards grinned. "Only thirty," he said. "I'm a lawyer. Entertainment personalities, TV, pictures."

"Would you believe?" Amanda said.

She meant that he looked like a film star. That didn't surprise Dave. Carl Brandstetter had looked like a film star too. But Carl Brandstetter had been sixty-five when Amanda married him. So what surprised Dave was Edwards's youth. He was still older than Amanda but not much. It was only a surprise. It wasn't important. What was important was that he earned a living and probably a good one. He wasn't after Amanda for her money.

Dave wasn't only old enough to be Amanda's father—he worried about her like a father. The way she had moped around that big, empty Beverly Glen house after Carl Brandstetter's sudden death had troubled him, and he'd tried to take her mind off her loss by putting her to work, remodeling and decorating the ramshackle place he'd bought to live alone in up Horseshoe Canyon. When that was done, he'd talked her into opening a business, and in no time she'd got more clients than she could handle, and was too busy to mourn. But he was uneasy that she seemed to shun all men except him, an aging homosexual. Now here she came with a man, and Dave was jealous. Ridiculous. He laughed at himself.

"Dave?" Amanda's eyes were bright. "We've got something to tell you."

But Mel Fleischer arrived, tall, balding, patrician, in dark green tweed, lavender shirt, pale green tie. He was a heavy contributor to the philharmonic and the museum, collected California painters, and was a senior vice-president of Proctor Bank. He and Dave had been lovers—

28

though that was a flowery word for it—in high school, when the world was young. They had remained friends. Trailing Mel came Makoto, the Japanese college boy he slept with, stocky, broad-faced. A shiny red jacket was open over his muscular brown torso. He wore red jogging shorts, white gym socks with red trim, and no shoes. Roller skates dangled from his square, brown hand—white tops, red wheels. From across the room, Max watched Makoto with a sad shake of the head, mourning a restaurant dress code long defunct.

Dave made introductions. Makoto sat down, dropped the skates on the thick carpet, lounged in the chair. Mel sat straight, a Renaissance cardinal holding audience.

Amanda told Makoto, "Those are beautiful skates."

Makoto nodded a head of shaggy black hair and showed terrific teeth. He didn't talk much. Spoken English was not easy for him. Amanda handed him her menu. Edwards tried to give his to Mel. Mel smiled and shook his head.

"Scallops," he said. "They sauté them beautifully here, in brown butter." He passed Dave an envelope. "The sad story of Charles Westover—financial only, but I often think a good novelist could reconstruct a whole life from a study of a man's bank statements, don't you?"

"Balzac," Makoto said. He pronounced it Borzock. *"César Birotteau."* The last name was easy for him.

Dave put on glasses and peered at the pages from the envelope. "Credit check here, too. Thanks. I see he's keeping up the house payments. Jesus, a third mortgage!"

"He'd better. But, as you can see, his debts elsewhere are staggering. In round figures, two hundred thousand dollars. The house and car are all he has."

29

"Ahem!" Amanda said. Dave laid down the papers and took off the glasses. She was holding Edwards's hand on the table, and she was radiant. "I have an announcement, please. Miles and I are getting married."

"Ho!" Dave was startled. She'd never kept a secret before. "Wonderful. Congratulations." He kissed her cheek and shook the hand of Edwards, who grinned happily.

"Champagne!" Mel waved his arms. "Champagne!"

4

At two in the morning, the sprawling, low-roofed houses along Sandpiper Lane were dark. He stopped the Triumph by the little palm again, and got out into wind as relentless as yesterday morning's wind but colder. The little palm rattled its fans. Far down the road, around a bend, a solitary streetlamp shone. Here it was very dark. He looked up. No moon. Not even stars. He went up the driveway toward the black bulk of the house. Leaves and pods crackled under his feet when he stepped up into the front-door recess. The eucalyptus smell was musty.

From his key case he chose one slim shaft of metal after another. The third worked in the lock but the door wouldn't open. There must be a dead bolt. He found his way along the side of the house, feeling with his hands. The brick was rough. He shuffled and went slowly. Twice he stepped up into the spongy yield of mulch in planters to test windows. Both were fastened. At the rear of the house was a roofed, screened patio. Its door was locked, would have been easy to open, but he didn't open it, figuring the door into the house itself would be bolted.

He went around front again, to the garage door. The padlock gave easily. Holding its pitted coldness in his hand, he turned and looked up and down the street. No one. He dropped the padlock into the pocket of his sheepskin jacket, bent, and lifted the garage door just enough to be able to slip under it. Inside, in the smells of dusty tires, grease, gasoline, he let the door drop shut softly. He put his face close to the dusty little pane. No one. He risked probing the darkness for a second with the beam of a penlight. Nothing lay for him to stumble over on his way to the house door. He switched the light off and went to the door. It was not locked. He stepped up and into the house and closed the door behind him.

He stood braced for bad smells, death, decay. He didn't smell anything like that. The air was warm. Westover or Lyle had forgotten to turn off the thermostat. He went toward the front of the house. He felt rather than saw a large room open to his right. As if blind, he walked a slow step at a time, silent on carpet. He groped out with his hands. He bumped furniture. Something flimsy and metallic fell with a delicate clatter. He waited. No one had heard. His hands found curved, polished wood. A piano? What he wanted to find were curtains. He found them. Drawn across their windows. He thought he remembered that from yesterday morning.

He risked using the penlight again. The curtains were drawn on all the windows. What he had mistaken for a piano was a harpsichord. On its closed top lay a flute and an oboe. Dust muted the shine of their wood, their metal. What he had knocked over was a music rack. There were two more, each with music open on it. He righted the fallen rack. Printed on the cover of the music was *Anton*

Reicha: Strings, Woodwinds, Continuo. He set it on the rack, which trembled with its weight. He touched a key of the harpsichord. It sang sweetly. The harpsichord had two manuals.

He listened. He followed the penlight's thin beam into all the rooms, closing the curtains, switching on lights. No one—alive or dead. One room was a den, an office—desk, typewriter, files. He left that to look at bedrooms. There were four. In two, the beds were unmade. Over one hung framed photographs, eight-by-tens, six of them, in two rows. He recognized Wanda Landowska in beaky profile at a keyboard. He peered at the signature on another photograph. Igor Kipnis—another harpsichordist. Bookshelves stood in this room. On them, elaborate stereo equipment shouldered record albums, untidy heaps of music, books about music, composers, performers. Nothing distinguished the other bedroom. In both, clothes lay folded in the chests of drawers, clothes hung in closets. Shoes. Luggage.

There were three large bathrooms lined with mirrors, but only one had the look of having been in use. Pressure cans of shave cream, tooth powder, toothpaste, a pair of toothbrushes, two plastic-handled throwaway razors. Why won't Westover be back tomorrow? Why won't the kid? Something red sparked in the shag weave of a bathmat. He bent for it. A capsule. He checked druggist's amber plastic vials in the medicine chest. No Seconals. But he thought this was a Seconal. In the kitchen a few unwashed dishes were stacked on a sink counter. On a breakfast bar like the one at Scotty Dekker's across the street, slices of dark bread had slumped from a clear plastic wrapper and dried out. A quarter-inch of milk had soured in the bottom of a tall glass. Butter had puddled in its oblong dish. Cheese slices were growing green mold in their open packet. A half-empty jar of mayonnaise gaped, its lid beside it. A fly had died in the mayonnaise. Ferns hung in baskets over the breakfast bar. The fronds were drying out and turning brown. He rinsed the milk glass at the sink and watered the ferns.

Back in the den, he sat in the chair that had a tall padded leather back and padded leather arms and that swiveled, could turn to the desk, could turn to the typewriter table. Typed sheets lay stacked on the desk, facedown. A half-typed sheet was in the typewriter. It was a late-model electric typewriter. He switched on a desk lamp and peered at the typing. It didn't make a lot of sense. Something about making sure the mark didn't telephone the bank. He turned over the stack of pages. *"Confessions of a Con Man,"* the top page read, "by Howie O'Rourke, as told to Charles Westover." Dave put on his glasses and leafed through the pages. An introduction claimed that O'Rourke knew every swindle cunning and greed had devised since time began, had worked most of them, and had spent years in prison for getting caught at it. This book was going to tell all—no one who read it could ever be flimflammed out of his hard-earned money again. Dave checked the rest of the typescript, didn't find anything about insurance frauds, laid the sheets back together, tapped the edges on the dusty desk-top to straighten them, laid the stack on its face again, and rose to look into a brown steel file cabinet. In a folder labeled with the title of the book he found copies of query letters to twenty publishers. The letters asked for an advance of $200,000. Twelve publishers had replied. Negatively. None had even made a counteroffer.

Dave heard a noise. Not the wind. He slipped the folder back, quietly closed the file drawer, and switched off the desk lamp. Taking off his glasses, he moved in the dark to the door of the den and stood there listening, straining to hear. He had turned off the lights in each of the rooms as he left it. His eyes strained against the darkness. What had the noise been? The garage door. It went up and down on armatures and these were equipped with big springs which sang baritone when they stretched. That was what he had heard faintly. But the house was dead quiet, the night, the neighborhood, except for the snore of the wind under the eaves and, far off, the surf. He waited, heartbeats thudding in his ears. He thought he heard the soft click of a door latch. He didn't listen for footfalls. There was all that thick carpeting. Then a girl's voice, tentative, timid, called:

"Lyle? Are you here?"

Light glowed at the end of the hall. He went toward it. He said, "Lyle isn't here." He came out into the room with the harpsichord. Lamps glowed in the room, and a girl was standing on the far side of the room, a fat girl whose hips bulged in too-tight jeans. Her big shoulders and bulky bosom were covered by a hand-loomed Mexican pullover, red, yellow, orange, with its hood laid back. She wore wire-rimmed, round glasses, and her hair was long, straight, straw-color. She looked surprised but not scared. He said, "Who are you?"

She said, "Who are you?"

"I'm an insurance investigator," he said, "and my name is Dave Brandstetter. Now it's your turn."

"Where's Lyle?" she said. "I keep phoning and no one answers. I keep coming. I need my flute and my oboe. Nobody answers the doorbell. So today I tried getting in.

35

Somebody phoned the security patrol. Luckily I saw them coming and ran around back and climbed the wall. If they'd found me I'd probably be in jail now. For attempted burglary. Are you going to call the police on me?"

"It would be the sheriff," Dave said, "and I've talked to the sheriff, and he doesn't want to come here."

"Everything was locked up tight," she said. "I was going to break a window tonight. Then I saw the lock was off the garage door. First I thought they were back, but their cars weren't here. You got the lock off, right?"

Dave took it out of his pocket and held it up.

She blinked. "Did you break it?"

"I didn't have to," he said.

"Where's Mr. Westover?" She tilted her head, puzzled. "Insurance? Did something happen to him?"

"I don't know. No one seems to know. I'm here because he filed an insurance claim with a company called Banner, only when I came to see him about it, he was gone. Appears to have been gone for days. I don't see the sense of that. Except that he was in financial trouble. Maybe he couldn't wait for his claim to be settled. What kind of trouble was Lyle in?"

"He couldn't go back to school." She went to the circle of glittering music racks. She crouched and brought out from under the harpsichord two leather-covered instrument cases and laid them open on the polished wood of the harpsichord. One case was lined with dark blue plush, the other with maroon-color plush. "He was working." She pulled the flute to pieces and laid the parts in grooves in one of the cases. "In the studios, TV background scores, you know—and recording studios. To help his father out." She pulled the oboe to pieces and laid its parts in the sec-

36

ond case. "He joined the union long ago, he was one of the youngest members. And good harpsichordists who can play classical, pop, rock, on sight, and tune their own instrument besides—they're not common, okay?" She closed the cases. "That was the only 'trouble' he had—that he couldn't go to school. He's got a lot of studying to do yet—or that's how he feels." She snapped the catches closed on the cases. "Can I show you something?" she said.

Dave went to her.

She turned the cases and with plump, dimpled fingers touched little metal tags riveted into the hard leather. Dave put on his glasses and peered through them at the tags. Each tag read "T. Foley." " 'T' is for Trio," she said. She was a homely girl. Her nose was a knob with a pushed-up tip like a pig's. She was too old for pimples but she had them. Her cheeks were balloons. The lenses in those wire frames that made her little eyes seem to swim were thick because one of the eyes was crossed. Her voice was colorless. Her mouth turned down at the corners. But she had a beautiful smile. "With a name like Trio"—she groped in a crossways pouch pocket in the front of the Mexican pullover—"what could I be but a musician?" She brought out a wallet whose leather lacing had come loose. She showed Dave her automobile operator's license, covered in cracked plastic that had turned yellow. "Trio Foley" was the name on the license, and the color photo made her look fatter than she was. She put the wallet away. "I wanted you to know I wasn't stealing someone else's instruments. Can I go now?"

"You can go without asking me," Dave said, "but I wish you'd tell me first where you think Lyle has gone."

"He didn't say he was going anywhere," she said. "If he

had, I wouldn't have left my instruments here, would I? The others took theirs, violin, cello. I had a score-copying job that wouldn't leave me time to practice. We were set up to meet here again Friday. No one was home. We couldn't understand it. Lyle was the one who set it up."

"Would they know where he went—violin, cello?"

"I doubt it," she said. "They didn't say so. And they hadn't known him long. Not like I have."

"Would he have gone with his father?"

She made a face. "He was here because he has a very strong sense of responsibility, and he owed his father, or thought he did, for all his father had done for him financially to see that he got a first-class musical education and all that. But he was just being dutiful. He'd lost all respect for his father after his father . . ." She eyed Dave nearsightedly through the thick lenses. "You know what his father did? You know he went to prison?"

"I know," Dave said.

"I don't mean Lyle said anything. He wouldn't. But you could tell how he felt—he never smiled at his father, all he said was yes and no, okay? I guess he felt sorry for him, in a way, but he really didn't"—she moved those big, square shoulders inside the Mexican pullover—"well, have any use for him. He was in—despair over him, all right?"

"There has to be love behind that," Dave said.

"He was here, wasn't he?" she said. "But he wouldn't run away with him—from the man's honest debts? Nothing like that."

"Do you know Howie O'Rourke?" Dave said.

"That creep," she said. "He used to hang around in here at night, pretending to listen to us, smoking grass, drinking wine. Red hair, long sideburns, and this dead white skin, you know? Fish-belly white? He thought he was God's gift to women. He didn't want to hear us play. He just wanted to have sex. With Jennifer, or Kimberly—even with me." She smiled wryly. "Can you believe that? He'd sprawl there on the couch with his legs stretched out, feeling himself up and leering at us. Really. Leering. Finally, Lyle told his father to keep him out of here."

"They were writing a book together," Dave said.

"Mr. Westover was writing it. Howie couldn't write his own name. He was telling Mr. Westover all his garbage about being a con artist." She snorted contempt. "Howie couldn't be a con artist. Howie couldn't be anything. Oh, maybe a worm—if he practiced a lot." She lifted music from one of the racks, made a thick roll of it, stuck the roll into the pouch pocket, and picked up the instrument cases from the harpsichord. She started off, then turned back. "If they went together, why are both cars gone?" She shook her head hard, and with certainty. Strands of the straw-color hair fell across her face. "They wouldn't go together." She stuck out her lower lip and blew at the fallen hair. "No way would they go together."

"Take this." Dave held out a card. "And if you get any ideas about where Lyle might be, telephone me, will you? Maybe something he said will come back to you, or something Mr. Westover said. I'll be grateful."

She tucked the flute case under her arm, took the card, glanced at it, stashed it away with the music, the wallet. "You know what I never thought? When I telephoned, and rang the doorbell and all that, and no one answered? That they could be in trouble. I was the only one I thought

39

about—getting my instruments." The hair flopped across her face again when she shook her head in disgust at herself. "I wasn't even worried about them. I should have told the police or someone that something was wrong here." Her crossed, magnified eyes apologized to Dave. "I'm not much of a human being, am I?"

"If you weren't," Dave said, "you wouldn't be worried about it. Is Lyle a close friend?"

"I've been in love with him since the first time we met. At Buenos Vientos, right? The music camp? We both had scholarships. It's for gifted kids, master classes, a good conductor. Summers. He was all alone in this empty practice cabin—they're just boards and two-by-fours, no glass in the windows. He was playing the piano. The sun was shining on him. He's very beautiful."

"He has a speech defect," Dave said.

"You don't notice that," she said, "not after while. It doesn't matter."

"Does he know you're in love with him?"

"Do you know any geniuses? He wouldn't notice. All he notices is music." Her laugh was sad.

"Can you be insensitive and be a good musician?"

"I'm fat, cross-eyed, and I have a bad skin," she said. "He doesn't know how I feel because I haven't told him. What would it be—just embarrassing for both of us, wouldn't it? He's not insensitive—just the opposite. You'll see. He's not childish—he's very intelligent and complicated, but there's something about him like a little boy, vulnerable. As soon as you meet him, you start to worry about him, wanting to shelter him, you know? Not when he's playing—he's fine then, strong. But the rest of the time, you can see things hurt him, see the pain in his eyes. And

40

you want to keep the pain away." She made a helpless little circle in the air with a plump hand. "I'm sorry. I can't explain it exactly. He looks so—fragile."

"Does he ever mention his sister?"

"Does he have a sister? Where is she?"

"Suppose he heard that she was dead, murdered," Dave said. "What would that do to him?"

She stared. She dropped the instrument cases on a long, low couch. They sank into deep brown velvet cushions. "Insurance," she said again. Her tongue touched her lips as if they were dry. "That's why you're here."

He told her what he knew. "What's your impression of Charles Westover?"

"Not that he'd do anything like that. He's like a ghost, gray, sad, kind of—shrunken. Oh, you can see just some- times what he must have been like, charming, funny. But mostly—I don't know—like he was—well, beaten."

"Did he know Lyle was fragile? Would he have told him that he thought Azrael had killed his sister?"

As if her legs wouldn't hold her, Trio dropped onto the couch. The instrument cases clunked together against her porky thigh. She sat hunched up, knees tight together, hands clutched tight in her lap. She stared at nothing. She said, almost to herself, "If he did, that's why Lyle isn't here. He ran away once before. He told me. I'd forgotten. It was before I knew him. When his father got caught. Lyle just left, disappeared. His mother had the police searching for him. It was in the papers, on TV—'Teen-age musical genius vanishes.' Then he came back. One day his mother walked in the door here, and he was taking a shower, just as if he'd never been gone."

"Did he tell you where he'd been?"

41

"No. It's not that he's secretive. That sounds sly, you know, and he's not sly, he's open as a child, as a flower. I guess it's just that it's so hard for him to make himself understood that, after while, he decided trying wasn't worth it. Not if you can play."

"Maybe he's gone back to New York," Dave said. "I'll phone Juilliard in the morning. It's possible they'll know some friend he's staying with there."

"Maybe he could fly on credit cards." She didn't sound as if she believed it. "But he didn't have any money. He turned it all over to his father." She rose and picked up the cases again. "As fast as the union sent him his checks."

"What kind of car does he have?" Dave said. "Would it get him to New York?"

"It wouldn't get him to Nevada." She went through the lamp shadows toward the entryway. "It's a beat-up old Gremlin. Junk." She turned back one more time. "Serenity? That's his sister's name? Ironical, isn't it?"

" 'Trio' made you a musician," Dave said. "Maybe her name saved her. Serenity can survive a lot."

She winced a little smile and went away. He listened for the hum of the garage-door springs. When he heard it, he switched off the lamps in the harpsichord room and went back to see what else he could find in Charles Westover's den.

5

The Triumph jolted over the hump from Horseshoe Canyon Trail and dropped sharply down into the brick-paved yard of his house. Only the head lamps lighted the yard. Amanda had installed ground spots in the shrubbery, but the rains of February had brought rushing mudslides down from the hills behind the place. Mud two feet deep had uprooted the lights and swept them off down the canyon with other debris—brush, trees, automobiles, parts of houses. Dave had got off lightly—warped floors, waterlogged furniture, soaked and swollen books. And the ground lights. He'd ordered replacements, but the contractor's waiting list was long.

The lights of the Triumph jittered, reflected in the square panes of the french doors that crossed the front of the building. They also showed him a vehicle he did not know—a new custom van, glossily painted with rearward streaking flames. He wheeled the Triumph in beside it, checked his watch—it was four-forty in the morning—shut off the engine, and climbed wearily out of the car. Who did he have to meet now? He wanted to sleep. The van's license frame named a Sacramento dealer. With the pen-

43

light, Dave probed inside the van through the windows. Nothing showed who owned it. A new road map lay on the seat.

He switched off the penlight, dropped it into the pocket of the sheepskin coat, and walked around the end of the building into the bricked center court where a big old live-oak loomed up blacker than the surrounding blackness. A wooden bench had been built around the thick trunk of the tree. Plants stood on most of the bench, but there was space to sit down. The brickwork on which the bench was footed was uneven, and the props of the bench clunked when it was sat on or stood up from. The props clunked now. Dave halted and groped for the penlight again.

"I guess you don't need me," a voice said, "not staying out till practically sunrise. You been in some warm bed, and it wasn't mine."

Dave found the penlight and poked its narrow beam at the sound of the voice. The beam showed him a tall, skinny young black in a leather cap, corduroy car coat with wooden peg fastenings, driving gloves. His name was Cecil Harris, and he stood with shoulders hunched, looking cold. His eyes were large in his thin face, and they expressed reproach.

Dave said, "I haven't been in a warm bed. I've been working. You know the kind of hours I have to keep." He put away the light, crossed the uneven bricks, took the boy in his arms and kissed him. They stood holding each other tight. "It's good to see you. How did you ever find me?"

"If you were on the moon," the boy said, "I would find you. You know that. Don't you know that?"

"I know it now." In Dave's arms, the boy shivered.

"Let's get you inside. How long have you been waiting? Why didn't you telephone?"

"I wanted to surprise you." Cecil chuckled though his teeth were chattering. "You know me and surprises."

"The last time"—Dave took his arm and walked him away from the tree—"you were also waiting in the dark. In my motel room at La Caleta. I thought you were a mugger. Nearly broke your arm with a wine bottle. Only that time you were naked."

Cecil shuddered audibly. "No way am I going to get naked in this weather. Not out here."

Dave unlocked a door—not to the front building, the one with the row of french windows. To a back building. This property was odd. Two stables it may have been once, each a single enormous room, and over yonder a cookshack. Amanda had redesigned them all, building here a roomy loft for sleeping, unfinished pine to match the original walls. Dave reached inside for a switch that lit a pair of lamps. The big room was chilly and still held a faint smell of damp and mud. Dave crouched to light, with a gas pilot jet, kindling and logs in a wide, used-brick fireplace, another of Amanda's improvements. When he rose, Cecil had not moved from inside the door. Dave said, "You're old enough so your brother couldn't stop you coming to me, so that means you're old enough for a drink. Brandy is warming. Would you like some brandy?"

Pulling off the driving gloves, Cecil came to the fireplace. He held his hands out to the logs that as yet were doing less flaming than smoking. "I was thinking," he said, "of another way to get warm. It's in the Boy Scout manual, you know? Rub two bodies together till you get a spark?"

He raised his eyes to the shadowed loft under its canted rafters. "That where the bed is?"

"It won't go away," Dave said. "I need a brandy, if you don't. It will make everything go better."

"No way we could go better," Cecil said. "We go the very best. I never forgot. I think about it every day, every night. Especially every night. I thought those eighteen months would never go by." A couch, pine frame, corduroy cushions, faced the fireplace. He dropped lankily onto it. "I went to your old digs, on Robertston, above the art gallery. This is strange, but that was stranger. You know how strange it was—all those big empty rooms?"

"Emptier than you think," Dave said.

"Christian was there, looking like he'd just barbecued Captain Cook. He wanted me out of my bulky winter clothes and into his hammock under the banyan tree."

"Where was Doug?" Dave said. He meant Doug Sawyer, with whom he had lived for a few years before the advent of Christian. Doug was a painter, but made his living from the gallery he owned. Christian ran a Polynesian restaurant across the street, the Bamboo Raft.

"Luckily, he came up the stairs before my virtue got violated. That is one big tropical fruit, that Christian. And Doug—he told me about this place. It took some finding. Hey, thank you." Dave had put into his long fingers a glass globe with two inches of Courvoisier in the bottom. The firelight glinted red in the brandy. Cecil studied it. "Pretty," he said, and tasted it. "Whoo-ee." He grinned up at Dave. "I see what you mean."

"What have you been doing?" Dave dropped onto the couch beside him, tasted his own brandy, lit a cigarette.

"You got into television, right?" When Dave had met him, Cecil was a trainee from a local college, getting on-the-job experience at a mountaintop station above a small city up the coast. "That's a nifty van. The pay must be good."

"Not in back of the camera," Cecil said. "Up Sacramento way. I wanted to come here, but you know my big brother, the jailer, who thinks gayness is something you outgrow. Shit, if I grow anymore, the basketball scouts won't leave me alone. No, the pay for behind the camera—typing up your tapes of highway-commission meetings—is not like the pay for looking pretty and mispronouncing words in front of the camera. No, I was gifted with some bread on my twenty-first birthday. That is how I come to have the van. I bought it yesterday." He checked a new watch studded with stops on his lean wrist. "Excuse me—day before yesterday."

"Happy birthday." Dave kissed his neat little ear.

"And I drove it straight to you. Well, maybe 'straight' is not the word I want. Maybe I mean, I drove it gaily to you, all right?" He laughed, sipped his brandy, grew solemn. His eyes were big and reproachful again. "Shit, I was scared when you didn't come. You don't know all the thoughts I had out under that tree. I was colder inside than I was outside. What if you forgot all about me? What if you didn't care anymore?"

"You didn't write," Dave said.

"I wrote," Cecil said, "I just never mailed what I wrote. It wasn't what you'd call decent, you know? I was writing with my cock. What good would that do you—what good did it do me?"

Dave snubbed out his cigarette. He stood and shed the

47

sheepskin coat. "It will be warm up in the loft now," he said. He picked up his glass, cigarettes, lighter, went into the shadows for the brandy bottle, went to the foot of the stairs. "You want to see how warm it is?"

Cecil unfolded his long bones from the couch, tossed the leather cap on the couch, dropped his car coat there. He came to Dave. "You could put it like that," he said.

The Juilliard School of Music had not Lyle Westover seen since nearly a year. That was how the young woman with the German accent who answered the telephone there put it. She was a student. It was not her job, answering this telephone. She had answered it because the office staff had left for the day. But she did know Lyle, and he had not last fall returned to Juilliard his classes to resume. She did not know whether he was with friends in New York staying, but she could not names of his friends give to strangers on the telephone. She did remember that he had a student instructorship been awarded for last summer at Buenos Vientos—that was in California. She hoped nothing bad to Lyle had happened.

"If he shows up," Dave said, "will you let me know, please?" He gave her his number, thanked her, hung the yellow receiver of the cookshack phone back in its place on the endboard of a knotty-pine cupboard. Corn bread was baking in the oven of the stately old steel-and-porcelain country kitchen stove Amanda had had refitted to run on gas. Heat leaked from the oven and made the cookshack pleasantly warm. He glanced out the window. Cecil came out of the rear building in a starchy new white robe with deep kimono sleeves. He was scrubbing his hair with a big

48

white bath towel. He stepped from the shadow of the live-oak into sunlight, turned his face up to the sun, blinking, feeling for warmth. Dave felt a sweet ache in his chest and turned away. It had been a long time since he had reacted to anyone this way. It was dangerous. Too many years separated them, decades. He was being a fool. He filled two yellow mugs with coffee and set them steaming on the country kitchen table Amanda had found in some junk-shop and stripped down to its original yellow pine. There were country kitchen chairs to match. The works of the refrigerator were new, but concealed in a gigantic old oak icebox of many doors.

"Thank God it's warm someplace." Cecil came in and shut the door. "This is southern California, man. Supposed to be desert. Keeps on like this, I will turn into a licorice Popsicle." He hung the towel over a chairback and sat down. "Ah, hot coffee." He took the mug in both hands. "Did you get New York? Something sure smells good."

"Corn bread," Dave said. "If you want to phone New York, you don't wait until two-thirty in the afternoon, Pacific standard time. You get out of bed like ordinary people."

"I liked it in bed," Cecil said.

"So did I," Dave said. The grille was ready, the eggs were beaten, the jack cheese was shredded, the avocado cut up. He made omelets. "I got somebody on the phone. I don't think Lyle is in New York." He bent and got the corn bread out of the oven. He lifted a corner of an omelet with a spatula. It was golden brown on the bottom. He folded both omelets. Burning his fingers, he cut generous slabs of the corn bread and let thick pats of butter melt into them.

He laid them in a basket with a yellow napkin over them and set the basket on the table. He slid the omelets onto plates, set the plates on the table. "To give you back your strength." He sat down across from Cecil. "Salt, pepper?"

"Look at that," Cecil said, and poked at the omelet with his fork. "What is *in* there, man?"

"Avocado," Dave said. "Cheese."

"Oh, wow." Cecil took a mouthful. His eyes widened. He opened his mouth and panted. "Hot!" he gasped.

"You wouldn't like it cold," Dave said. He pushed the basket of corn bread at him. "You want to play detective with me today? Or have you things to do?"

"Only thing I have to do is you," Cecil said. "Forever. From now on. All right?"

"All right." Dave smiled. "But I won't hold you to it."

"Hold me," Cecil said, "any way you want. Only the last time I played detective with you, you nearly got killed. That big dude with the beard on the smuggling boat?"

"There's no way you can take the blame for that," Dave said. "That was my own mistake."

"I shouldn't have left you by yourself," Cecil said. "I won't ever leave you by yourself again. This is better corn bread than Mama used to make."

"Ground the dried corn herself, did she?" Dave said. "Down on the old plantation?"

"Up in old Detroit," Cecil said. "Got it out of a ready-mix box from the supermarket. You add milk and an egg. No—she didn't have time to cook much. Always working. Working till it killed her. To turn my holy brother into a dentist, to buy me that van when I got to be twenty-one. What kind of case are you working on that kept you out till five in the morning?"

Dave told him. By the time he had finished, the plates were empty, the breadbasket was empty, they were drinking second mugs of coffee and smoking cigarettes. Dave took from a pocket of his blue wool shirt a flimsy pink form, rumpled, a carbon copy, smudged. He unfolded it and pushed it across the table to Cecil. "That was what I found—not in the files, on the desk. Westover rented a truck. If I'm right—on the very day he disappeared."

"If he took his Rolls-Royce"—the cigarette hung in a corner of Cecil's mouth, tough-detective style; he narrowed his eyes against the smoke while he read the form, and he used a Bogart voice—"what did he want with the truck?"

"Get dressed," Dave said, "and we'll try to find out."

Cecil got up. "Come with me while I dress."

"If I did, we'd never get out of here," Dave said.

The man behind the counter was a woman old and gray. The lines of the nonsense rhyme jumped into his mind and he had to suppress a grin in the storefront office of Momentum Truck Rentals in Santa Monica, where the walls were woodgrain plastic, and the plants that hung in baskets or crouched in corners were plastic. The woman in charge was a caricature little old lady, frail, in a doubleknit lavender pants suit stiff as cardboard. But he had no right to grin. He was gray himself and, if not as old as she was, still old. Cecil was making him forget that, making him remember that silly verse from his childhood. He showed the woman the pink flimsy.

"He didn't bring it back." She piped, she quavered.

"You mean he owes you money on it?"

"I mean he abandoned it," she said. "If you *read* this"—she tapped the flimsy with a bony finger—"you'll see he said he was going to return it the next day. Well, he didn't return it the next day. He never returned it, just climbed out of it and left it."

"You know that?" Dave said. "How do you know that?"

"Because we notified the police, sheriff, highway patrol. A prowl car spotted it, notified us, and we had it back here, noon the following day."

"Did he come in alone?" Dave said. "Were you on duty?"

"He had a boy with him." The twang of guitars crashed from a loudspeaker in a corner over a pair of chairs and a plastic veneered table. She looked up at the speaker. She trembled back to a woodgrain plastic door, yanked it open, and shrilled into a room where a long-haired youth in a ten-gallon hat sat with his feet on a desk, munching a hamburger, "Turn that racket down. I have people out here." She slammed the door and came back. The guitars faded to a whisper. "Skinny, curly-headed boy," she went on, as if nothing had happened. "Man's son, I guess. Looked like him, a little. Had something wrong with him. Couldn't talk right."

"Why did he talk at all?" Dave said.

"I don't think he wanted the man to rent the truck," she said. "Hard to understand him, mouth full of marbles. I did catch one thing, though. Says, 'If you do this, you're no better than O'Rourke.' Reason I remember the name, my first husband was an O'Rourke. Dead now." She frowned, folded the pink slip, handed it back to Dave. "No, the boy was angry, nervous. While I made up the papers, he kept walking out like he was going to leave, just have nothing to do with it—but he always came back in after a minute."

"Did Westover pay in cash?" Dave asked.

"Most people use credit cards," she said, "but he had cash."

"Did you notice what kind of car he came here in?"

"Couldn't help it, could I?" she said. "Rolls-Royce, vintage. Now, you see your share of Rollses, especially if you drive through Beverly Hills, which I do, coming in to work every day from the Valley. But they don't often show up here. People like that don't rent trucks. They get their furniture hauled by moving companies."

"Did he say he was moving?" Dave asked.

"He didn't say what he was doing," she said. "It's none of my business. I wondered, of course. Guess I wondered out loud, but he didn't say. Not that I remember. He made the boy drive the truck, he followed in the Rolls."

"Where did they abandon the truck?" Dave said.

She turned to a computer keyboard and punched up the information. It came in cross-stitch letters on a television screen encased in grubby white plastic. "El Segundo." She read off a street address. She smiled at Cecil. She had pearly little false teeth. "What are you so happy about? I swear, you're grinning all over yourself."

"Just married," Cecil said, and bent double, and spun around, laughing. When he recovered himself, she made him a present, a tiny toy truck with MOMENTUM printed on its side.

The address was off the San Diego freeway in an area of lonely warehouses, abandoned rows of shops, weedy vacant lots strewn with automobile carcasses. Now and then an oil pump cast a nodding shadow in the long, late afternoon winter sunlight. Where people lived, existed, were clutches of shacks, broken-windowed, porches falling off, roof gaps showing fishbones of gray rafter. Black children in gaudy rags ran the cracked sidewalks, sick old black people hobbled, sick dogs dodged and slunk. In patches of shade among the rotting cars, tattered men sprawled, snoring openmouthed, clutching empty wine bottles.

"Soweto," Cecil said.

"You can't see this from the freeway," Dave said.

"They landscape that, don't they?" Cecil said. "Shit, you're driving through the real America, and you don't even know it. Green groundcover, flowering bushes, lacy trees. Fucking paradise. Here's the street." He steered the van away from the shacks, the blacks. Not a sound here. Grass sprouting through the asphalt. Bleak storage buildings—some of them cinderblock, the paint of sign lettering flaking, fading; some of them corrugated iron, the bolts weeping rust. It was one of these he stopped at. "This is it."

They climbed down out of the van. Shadows of gulls flickered over them. In the distance a ship's whistle sounded hoarsely. Again. They stared at the building. It had a loading dock and broad doors hung by wheels to a rusty rail. No one had used the loading dock or the doors in a very long time. Seasons of bramble crops had grown and withered in front of the dock. They crackled through the dead brambles and climbed plank stairs. At the far end of the doors was a window. They went to it and tried to see inside. The window was crusted with salt from the sea air. Dave spat on his fingers and rubbed some of the crust away. He put his face to the glass. Cobwebs that had trapped only dust were thick on the inside of the window. He wasn't sure of what he saw but it looked like emptiness.

"We could break it," Cecil said. "Nobody would know."

Dave went to examine the place where the doors came together. Hasps held padlocks, corroded, one at waist level, one at shoe-top level. "Tire iron?" he asked Cecil. Cecil fetched a brand-new tire iron. Dave pried the hasps loose on the top lock. Cecil wedged the iron under the other hasp, yanked, and it came loose too. Dave gripped the edge of the right-hand door and pulled. There were rusty squeaks up on the roller rail but the door didn't budge. Cecil took hold of the door with him and they hauled at it together. It didn't yield.

"I'm going to smash out that window," Cecil said.

"I think I saw a door along the side," Dave said.

They trudged through weeds—last year's tall, brown, brittle; this year's short, feebly green; trash in the weeds, beer cans, dusty wine bottles—between this building and the next. The passageway was cold, as if the sun never reached it. Dave climbed plank steps to a rickety stoop that trembled under him. The door was thin, an ordinary room door, old. He tried the gritty knob. The door was locked. He stepped back and aimed a kick with his heel just below the knob. The door didn't fly open. Instead, one of its panels fell out with a clatter that echoed. He knelt.

"Don't go in there," Cecil said. "Let me do that."

Dave poked his head inside. The light was poor but there was enough to show him the place was empty. He withdrew his head. "Never mind," he said. He got to his feet and descended the steps, brushing dirt off his hands, off the knees of his pipestem corduroys. "There's nothing in there—not even a broken crate."

"What did they bring that truck here for?" Cecil said.

Dave headed for the sundown street. Cecil followed. Dave said, "Lyle can tell us."

"You said you don't know where he is."

Dave opened the van door. "I've changed my mind," he said. "Tomorrow, we'll go ask him."

Cecil slouched in a deep chair alone in a far corner of the room and watched the news on television. At this end of the room were laughter, the tinkle of ice in glasses, the munching of *dim sum*. Amanda and Miles Edwards had brought the food, warm in foil, and had unwrapped it in the cookshack. It was being consumed in the long front building of Dave's place, which Amanda had made interesting by raising and lowering floor levels, expanding the fireplace, and adding clerestory windows so daylight could get in, because Dave refused to cut the trees that surrounded the place. It was past seven, yellow lamplight bloomed softly in the room, there were bays of velvety shadow, and the trees couldn't be seen now through the french windows.

What could be seen, reflected in the small square panes, were strangers who belonged to Edwards and Amanda—young fair faces, middle-aged glossy faces, vaguely familiar from television shows that depended for laughs on pratfalls and odd costumes—and friends who belonged to Dave. Mel and Makoto. Ray Lollard, plump and matronly, a telephone-company executive who sometimes helped Dave out with numbers hard to get, had brought Kovaks in clay-stained workclothes and two days' beard stubble. Kovaks was a potter who had set up shop in a stable back of Lollard's expensively restored 1890s mansion on West

56

Adams, and who seemed to make Lollard happy. A lean, dark, intense man talked with Amanda. He was Tom Owens, an architect Dave had narrowly saved from being murdered a few years back. Doug Sawyer, neat and slight, chatted with a pair of young actors. Happily, Christian hadn't come. Madge Dunstan stood with Dave—bony, freckled, her honest laughter showing long, horsey teeth. She was a very old friend, a successful designer of fabrics and wallpapers, an unsuccessful lover of beautiful young women whom she never could hold on to for long. Tonight's was tall, blond, boyish, famous from television commercials for a shampoo.

Dave hadn't caught her name. Nor was he listening to her while she talked at him. He was pretending to listen. He was watching the back of Cecil's skull, which he could just see above the chairback far away in shadow, the TV tube a bright kaleidoscope beyond him. He wondered if Cecil was sulking, and if so why. He had been merry fifteen, twenty minutes ago, enjoying everybody, everybody enjoying him. He had spent some minutes by the fireplace talking to Edwards. Dave had been occupied with mixing and handing out drinks and hadn't paid attention. But he remembered that they hadn't smiled, that they'd seemed earnest. Now Edwards was laughing, arm around Amanda, who was laughing with him. They looked fine together—handsome, happy, young. He wasn't worried about Amanda anymore.

But he didn't understand Cecil. Yes, television news enchanted him. Before he had met Dave, he wanted to be part of it. Dave went down two waxed pine steps, crossed Navajo rugs, went up pine steps. A glass hung in Cecil's long fingers, but he hadn't touched the drink in it. On the television screen was film from a handheld camera that bobbed, panning the stumbling progress of a young man in yellow coveralls, handcuffs, chains on his ankles, being led past a gray wall by uniformed officers. His hair was long and yellow and needed combing. He had a tangled yellow beard and blue eyes that glared savagely at the camera lens. Dave sat down in the chair beside Cecil, took the drink from his hand, sipped at it, and bent forward to hear the voice of the talking head that had replaced the jittery film. The sound was low. . . . "was released by Tucson authorities late this afternoon, when his real identity was established. . . ." Dave switched off the set.

Cecil looked at him, as if only now realizing he was there. He said, "They thought they had Azrael for sure. Looks just like him. Wrong man." He shivered. "Those eyes, though. This one's got to be crazy too."

"There are different kinds of crazy," Dave said. "Happily most of them don't murder girls and bury them in the backyard."

"This one's never even heard of Azrael." Cecil shook his head in wonder and disgust. "He never sees the news, never reads. He watches the clouds and the birds, the little streams rippling over the pretty rocks, right? He listens to the wind in the trees, and watches the sunrise."

"They'll get him for that eventually," Dave said. He handed Cecil back his glass. "Are you all right?"

"I can't go with you tomorrow." Cecil didn't look at him. He talked to the blank television screen. "I've got an appointment. For a job." He took a quick gulp of whiskey.

Dave blinked and felt bleak. "When did all this happen?

58

You were going to work with me, you were never going to leave me by myself again. Isn't that what you said? This is pretty sudden, isn't it? What do you need with a job?"

"You don't want a kept boy," Cecil said.

"Will you look at me, please? What the hell are you talking about? You'll earn your keep."

Cecil shook his head impatiently. "You don't need my help. You don't need anybody's help. Got along fine on your own all this time. Kept boy, that's what I'd be." He jerked his head to indicate the laughing people at the other end of the room. He pitched his voice up, pursed his mouth, fluttered his lashes. " 'What do you do, young Cecil? Do you act, do you interior decorate, do you style women's hair?' " He changed voices. " 'No, ma'am—ah jus' sleeps with Mistuh Brandstettuh.' "

"Edwards put this idea into your head," Dave said.

"He just figured I'd be wanting a job, and he's fixing it for me. A good job. Field reporter. On camera."

"You didn't want that anymore," Dave said.

"It will keep me honest." Cecil was big-eyed, imploring. "It won't change anything between us. Just, I can't be with you all the time. Don't they say that's best?"

"I don't know who they are," Dave said, "but Edwards is an interfering bastard." He stood up, turned, and Edwards was watching from across the room. Dave couldn't read his expression. Not smug. What the hell was it? Anxious?

Cecil tugged Dave's wrist. "Don't spoil it. It will be a good job, the pay will be great, it will make me feel righteous, like I was somebody fit for you to love."

"You were that before," Dave said.

"If you care how I feel," Cecil said, "you will sit down.

59

If all you care about is knocking Edwards upside his head, go on."

Dave sat down. "I care how you feel," he grumbled.

"I couldn't just live off you," Cecil said gently. "You know that wouldn't be right."

"I wish they'd go the hell home," Dave said, "so I could get you to bed and talk some sense into you."

6

It was lonely country, lifting gently toward ragged mountains through low hills velvet with new green from winter rains, hills strewn with white rocks and clumps of brush, and slashed here and there by ravines dark with big live-oaks. An eight-lane freeway had brought him into the hills from the seacoast, forty clean, sleek miles of new cement leading God knew where, nobody driving it but him, under low-hanging clouds, dark and tattered, spattering the windshield with squalls of rain one minute, the next minute letting shafts of sunlight through.

He began to pass vineyards that striped the hills, then shaggy groves of avocado, leaves and limbs drooping from the heaviness of the rain. He rolled down the window of the Triumph to breathe the clean air, the smell of rain on soil. Rain touched his face. A meadowlark sang. He wished that Cecil were with him. Then here was the green-and-white road sign warning him that Buenos Vientos could be reached by taking the next off-ramp. The off-ramp was a graceful, broad curve, but it brought him to a meager strip of worn and winding blacktop.

This climbed out of the groves, the vineyards, into the first and least of the mountains. Patches of snow began to show under clumps of brush and to the lee sides of rock outcrops. The sky darkened and the good winds for which the place was named turned mean, buffeting the little car, chilling him. He rolled up the window. After a while, he came among pines, scrubby at first, scattered, twisted by winds—then growing closer together, straighter, taller. They sheltered the little town. A clutch of shake-sided houses, a fieldstone filling station, a raw plank stable that rented out horses, a general store and post office with a long wooden covered porch, a bat-and-board café, BEER in small red neon in a window. From between the pumps of the filling station, a white-eyed husky barked at the Triumph as it passed.

The music camp was five miles farther on, a loose collection of raw pine buildings in a meadow. One of the buildings was large, two-storied, with glass in its windows —probably the dormitory and mess hall. The rest were one- or two-room practice sheds. Downhill beyond a screen of pines could be seen the lofting wooden arc of an orchestra shell. A faded, dented Gremlin stood under a big ponderosa pine beside the farthest of the practice sheds. Snow lay under the car. Dave pulled the Triumph up behind it and got out stiffly into the cold air.

He looked through the doorway into the little building. No piano, not now. A sleeping bag in a far corner, propped beside it a duffel bag, flap open. He turned and looked all around the little meadow. No sign of anyone. He called Lyle Westover's name. It came back to him in echoes from the silent slopes. He poked his head into the other practice sheds. Empty. His heels knocked hollowly when he climbed to the log-railed porch of the main building. From their solidity when he pounded on the plank double doors, he judged they were barred. Vacant rooms sent back the noise of his fists.

The car was unlocked. Nothing unexpected, nothing that gave answers. In the shed, he rummaged through the duffel bag—underwear, sweaters, wool shirts, corduroys. Also cans—baked beans, beef stew, Spam, a jar of instant coffee, crackers, a roll of toilet paper. Fifty feet behind the shed, charred sticks lay on a circle of blackened stones. The bottom of the gray enamel coffee pot was smoky. Pine needles floated in an inch of coffee in a gray enamel cup. In an unwashed steel skillet lay an unwashed steel fork. Downhill, a patch of duff had been scraped away. He dug there with a fallen pine branch. The hole held empty cans, labels still fresh. Snow began to fall on them. He covered them and went back to the shed. The sleeping bag was heavy when he picked it up. When he shook it, a pair of boots fell out. Dave scowled. Where the hell could he have gone in his stocking feet?

He stepped down out of the shed. The snow was falling harder now. "Lyle!" he shouted, "Lyle!" and headed for the orchestra shell. He turned up the sheepskin collar, hunched his shoulders, jammed his hands into the jacket pockets. He went down the center aisle, looking along the rows of pine-log benches. He hiked himself up on the stage, the cement cold to his hands. Doors—to storage rooms, dressing-rooms?—opened at either side of the shell, but they were padlocked. He used the shell to amplify his voice and shouted Lyle's name out into the snowfall. It sounded very loud in his ears, but no answer came. His ears were so cold they ached. He covered his ears with his hands and climbed back up the aisle. At the top, he shouted the boy's name again, once to each point of the compass. He thought of following his voice out among the big pines. But the snow fell in dense earnest now. It was hard to see through. One man didn't make a search party anyway—not in country this big and empty. One man could get lost and freeze to death. He went back to his car.

In the little town, the windows of the café smiled yellow through the snowfall. It was only noon, but the snowfall made it dark. He parked beside a battered pickup truck and entered the café through a door hung with little bells that jingled. The air inside was warm, steamy, and smelled of cooking. A pair of leathery men, one old, one young, both in cowboy hats and quilted khaki jackets, sat at a counter shoveling down meatloaf, mashed potatoes, gravy, green peas. Thick white mugs of coffee steamed in front of them. They glanced at Dave and away again, seeing he was a stranger.

A plump, motherly-looking woman in a starchy print dress, new cardigan sweater, patched white apron, chatted through a service window with someone unseen in the kitchen. She looked at Dave with more interest than the customers had done. Dave laid a bill on the counter. "Can I have a cup of coffee and change, please, for the telephone?" It was screwed, black and battered, to the wall at the far end of the room. The woman took the bill and jangled open the cash register. She laid coins in his hand. She gave him a lovely false-teeth smile.

"You look half frozen," she said. "You drove through only an hour ago. I thought then you'd be cold. It's that cloth top. That's a cute little car, but you can't expect to keep warm in it. Not in Buenos Vientos in the winter."

"The coffee?" Dave begged.

"Coming right up."

The directory that hung on a chain off the phone was tattered, dog-eared, food-stained, but he found the San Diego county offices section and a number that looked as if it might be the right one. The motherly woman brought a mug of coffee to the end of the counter and set it there for him. She didn't go away. She stood watching him with open curiosity. The phone kept ringing at the far end, and Dave stretched to try to reach the coffee mug. She picked it up and handed it to him. He burned his mouth on the coffee. It had come out of an ordinary café glass pot but it tasted like farmhouse coffee. The heat of it made him shiver. He was colder than he'd realized. At last a voice came on the line.

"Sheriff station, Guzman speaking."

Dave gave his name, said he was an insurance investigator, and wanted to report a missing person. "From the music camp at Buenos Vientos." Yes, he knew it was closed, but this boy had been holed up in one of the sheds. "His gear is all there—clothes, even boots—and his car is there, but he's nowhere around. It's snowing hard up here. Somebody ought to try to find him. The name? Lyle Westover, age about nineteen, slight build. He—" A hand tugged Dave's shoulder and he turned. The motherly woman was shaking her head.

"Don't bother them," she said.

"Sir?" the voice on the line said. "Are you there?"

"Yes, just a second." Dave covered the mouthpiece. He asked the woman what she meant.

"Isn't he the little one that can't talk right?" she asked. Dave nodded. She said, "I thought so. You get to know them all here in the summer."

"You know where he is—is that what you're saying?"

"In the hospital at Cascada," she said.

Dave said into the telephone, "I'm sorry. False alarm. I'm at the café here in town. They've located him for me. Excuse the trouble."

"No problem, sir." The line went dead. Dave hung up.

"At least," the woman said, "I guess that fat girl took him to the hospital. She come running in here, asking where the nearest one was. I know her too. Trio, they call her." She laughed. "I guess because she's bigger than any three of the rest of them."

"When was this?" Dave said.

"Said she had somebody in the car very sick, and she had to get them to a hospital right away. Last night, around six. Busy in here. But she was scared, plain to see that. I told her the way to Cascada. She was so jittery, I wasn't sure she took in what I said. She was out that door before the words were hardly out of my mouth. I ran after her to yell the directions to her all over again, and that was when I saw who it was that was sick. Passed out cold, head over against the window glass. Oh, he was pale, white as a ghost, blue around the mouth. Frail little thing, anyway, you know."

Dave drank more of the scalding coffee, set the mug down. "She hasn't come back, of course?"

66

"She went up first in the morning. I saw her pass, saw her come down too, not more than an hour after. She tore right on through, lickety-split. I guess I was busy when she drove up there the second time. Never saw her. Then, of course, here she came, barging in wild-eyed, out of breath. Quick—where was the nearest hospital?"

"Thanks," Dave said. "Where is it?"

Cascada huddled dreary in cold rain. Its Main street storefronts were red brick, brown brick. Feed and grain, hardware, drugstore. Modern crisp-lettered white plastic signs gleamed, so did the windows at McDonald's and the Pizza Hut, but no one was around, and the effect was sad. He found the hospital at the end of Main street, where the motherly woman had told him it would be—a new, sand-color stucco building with a white rock roof, one story, maybe twenty rooms. The lawn around it was bright with new grass, the plantings of eucalyptus trees young and lacy. He left the Triumph on the new blacktop of a parking lot almost empty, glossy with rain. Plate-glass doors led him into a shiny little reception area. An elderly nurse pointed him down a hallway. In the hallway, he found Anna Westover, seated on a stiff, minimally upholstered armchair, and looking drawn and bitter.

"What are you doing here?" she said.

"I told you I was looking for him," Dave said.

"He's in a coma," she said. "He tried to kill himself with sleeping pills. God, that child, that child." Her voice shook. On the big, soft leather bag in her lap, her thin hands clutched each other so tightly the knuckles shone white. She was angry—at Lyle, or at herself? "What in the world is the use?" It was a cry from the heart. She looked up at Dave with tears in her eyes. "You struggle to raise them, to understand them, to make life easy for them, to train them not to make the stupid mistakes you've made. And what in the world is the use?"

"If you did all that," Dave said, "you don't have anything to reproach yourself for. He's a big boy now." He sat down on another of the stingy chairs. A low table was between the chairs, on it a jug-shape terra-cotta lamp, old copies of *Westways* and *Sunset* magazines, a terra-cotta ashtray glazed blue inside. "What does the doctor say?"

"That he'll probably be all right." She muttered it, rummaging in the big bag for tissues, wiping her eyes, blowing her nose. "But what's to stop him trying it again? If life is so terrible for him?" A squeaky sob jerked out of her. She drew breath sharply, bit her lip, shook her head, squared her shoulders. "Did you find his father?"

"No. I hoped Lyle could tell me where to do that." Down the hallway, crockery and metal clashed. A bald, red-faced orderly in rumpled white brought trays out of rooms and dumped them into rubber bins on a trolley. Dave lit a cigarette. "Trio Foley brought him here. Where is she?"

"Eating," Anna Westover said flatly. "Every hour on the hour. It comforts her, I suppose. She feels terribly guilty, poor thing. She blames herself."

He had been mistaken in thinking the Pizza Hut was empty. She sat at a rear table whose shiny orange top, reflecting into her face, made the pimples stand out. A wheel of pizza lay in front of her, heaped with, as the white plastic letters of the sign over the counter put it, EVERY-

THING. Three wedges of the pizza were already gone and she was choking down a fourth. Dave sat across from her.

"Oh, God." Her eyes opened behind the thick glasses.

"I thought you were going to telephone me."

She gulped the mouthful of dough and sauce, cheese, sausage, anchovies. She drank from a big wax-paper cup of cola. Tomato sauce smeared her mouth and chin. She wiped them with a wadded fistful of paper napkins. She said, "I was afraid you'd frighten him."

"Why? I didn't frighten you."

Her dimpled fingers fumbled loose another slice of pizza. She lifted it toward her mouth. He caught her wrist.

"Wait a minute with the eating, please? Tell me what happened. He'd been living up there at the camp, cooking and eating and getting along. Then you showed up, and he swallowed Seconals. Now, what's it all about, Trio?"

"I told him." Her cry ricocheted off the shiny glass and plastic of the empty place. The blond boy and girl in uniform behind the counter stopped chatting and stared. "I went to make him leave there before you could find him but he didn't want to. Then I did just what I was afraid you'd do. I didn't mean to, but one thing led to another. Why had I come, and who were you, and what were you doing at the house, and why were you an insurance investigator, and—and—it all just came out, you know? About his father and his sister and the insurance and—" She couldn't go on. She picked up the pizza wedge and stuffed her face with it and sat there with tears streaming down her face, chewing, chewing.

"And then you ran away," Dave said, "leaving him all by himself with the knowledge that either his sister had been horribly murdered, or his father was so rotten that he had tried to defraud the insurance people by pretending he believed that had happened. Good Christ, girl, you were the one who said he was fragile, who wanted to protect him."

"Stop it!" She clapped her hands to her ears. "Stop it!" She had to wriggle mightily to free her bulk from the cramped space between table and banquette, but she did it with surprising quickness, and was on her feet and running for the door, all jiggling two hundred pounds of her, wailing like a siren. Dave sighed, got up, walked after her.

"Hey, mister, wait a minute." It was the blond boy behind the counter, rosy-cheeked, maybe seventeen but brave. "What happened? What did you do to her?"

"Gave her bad news," Dave said, "not gently enough."

The boy looked doubtful. He glanced at the blond girl. She nodded toward an orange telephone gleaming on a kitchen wall. Dave didn't wait for them to call the police. He pushed out into the rain and trudged after the wide, wobbling figure of Trio running away from him down the sad, empty street. When he caught up to her, she was hunched in a hospital hallway chair, trying to stop crying, Anna Westover bending over her, murmuring comfort. The woman glared at Dave.

"You bring joy wherever you go," she said.

"Trio," Dave said, "you saved his life. The mistake doesn't count. You fixed it. He's going to be all right."

She looked up at him, reproachful, face sleek with tears, glasses smeared with tears. She hiccuped. "I'm still hungry," she said, and burst out crying again.

He did look fragile, as if the least little tap would shatter him. Against the hospital pillows, his thin face was sickly

70

pale, with a stubble of dark beard. His hair curled, soft as a child's, on his elegant skull. His eyes were large, brown, sorrowful. As Trio had said, he was beautiful, and looking at him made you want to shelter him. Yet his wide, mobile mouth was able to smile. The smile was sheepish for the trouble he'd caused, but it was real.

Dave was alone with him now. He had left the hospital at midnight, checked into a motel, tried to telephone Cecil and got no answer, had slept hard anyway. He'd headed back here through gray drizzle at seven. Passing the steamy plate glass of bright McDonald's, he had glimpsed Trio stowing away scrambled eggs and muffins. He'd met Anna Westover wearily crossing the hospital parking lot to her car, on her way back to L.A. to look after other people's children. She told him Lyle was awake, out of danger, calm, apologetic, and able to talk—if that was the word for it.

From the look of the tray beside Lyle's bed, he'd been able to eat. His talk came out mostly vowels. Dave looked around for paper and pencil so the boy could write his answers. Pencil and paper were there none. So he strained to understand, and before long, he didn't have to ask Lyle to repeat—at least not everything.

"The cap came off, and they spilled all over the bathroom," he was saying now. "I was in a hurry to get out of there, away from him. I almost left the pills. But I felt like dying. I was so ashamed. And I knew him. He'd do something even worse next time. I didn't want to know about it. So I picked them up and put them in my pocket."

"But you changed your mind at the camp."

"It's beautiful there, and far away, and quiet. I could think. Why should I take them? Whatever I did, he'd go on

71

trying to save himself any dirty way he could. I wouldn't change him by dying. I was getting ready to go home. Then Trio showed up, and told me this thing he'd done about Serenity, and I got hysterical again, and she got scared and ran, and I took the pills. I began to get very cold, and I crawled into the sleeping bag, and I was drifting off, and I realized I still had my boots on. It seemed very important to get those boots off. And that's the last I remember." He tried to smile at himself.

"You got them off," Dave said. "Tell me—what had your father done to make you so ashamed? You and he rented a truck that night. Was that part of it?"

Lyle said two words. Dave couldn't make them out. He must have looked blank, because Lyle repeated them, slowly, working his beautiful mouth, frowning with the effort. "Howie O'Rourke. You know about him?"

"He and your father were writing a book," Dave said.

"Publishers kept turning it down," Lyle said. "It wasn't going to get him the money he wanted."

"You were giving him money," Dave said.

Lyle made a face. "After the house payments we were lucky to have anything left over for food. He had to have two hundred thousand dollars. Thought he had to."

"To clear the title to the house," Dave said, "so he could sell it and get out from under. Explain the truck."

"Howie found a way to get the money. Crooked, of course. He'd run into a man he'd known in prison, who had a truckload of hijacked stereo equipment he couldn't sell himself because the police were watching him."

"Excuse me," Dave said. "A truckload of what?"

It took a minute, but Lyle made him understand.

"There was two hundred thousand dollars worth of it, hidden in an old warehouse. The man only wanted twenty thousand for it."

"Only? Did your father have that kind of money?"

"No." Lyle looked at the rainy window. Tears started down his face. "That was what made me want to die. He got it from Don Gaillard." He drew a long, wobbly breath.

"I don't know who that is," Dave said.

"The nicest man that ever walked," Lyle said. "My father's oldest friend. When I was little, I thought he was my uncle. He wasn't. They were just very close—in high school, college, law school." Lyle's hands lay on the coverlet, which was threadbare, bleached from too many washings. The beautiful thin fingers moved, running silent scales. He watched them for a moment, then gave Dave a wan smile. "I wasn't too happy when I was small. My father was very busy making money. And my mother never forgave me for not being able to talk right. Oh, she tried not to let it show, but I knew. I was really surprised to see her here."

"She wants you to live, she wants you to be happy."

"That's not easy, is it?" Lyle said.

"Not for her," Dave said, "not when you act this way."

"I didn't think. It was my father who was on my mind. Did you admire your father?" When Dave nodded, Lyle said wryly, "So did I. Then there wasn't anything to admire anymore." He drew another shaky breath. "Anyway, I loved Don. He had time for us. We loved having Don come over."

"So he was almost a member of the family," Dave said. "Why shouldn't your father go to him for a loan? Isn't that what friends are for, to be there when we need them?"

"Only they hadn't been friends—not for years and years. The break was sudden. Serenity and I couldn't understand. Where was Uncle Don? And they told us to forget Uncle Don, never mention Uncle Don again. I was too young to understand, but I figured out after while that Don must have told my father he didn't like the way he was going—criminal law, all that. He got out of law himself, began building furniture in his basement. Which made him poor, too, didn't it? At least not like the crowd my parents were in, the beach club, all that. Big cars. The best of everything. Old Don just didn't belong, did he?"

"They hadn't spoken in years?"

"That's it." Lyle nodded disgust. "I couldn't believe my father would be so creepy. Don isn't rich. He works hard for his money, works with his hands."

"But he had it," Dave said, "and he gave it?"

"Gladly. He'd give my father anything. That's how Don is. The kindest man, the kindest man. It probably was every cent he'd saved in his life."

"So you went to the warehouse with the truck and Don Gaillard's twenty thousand dollars to pick up the loot."

"Not the money. My father had already passed that to Howie to pay his jailbird friend. Howie was supposed to meet us at the warehouse."

"Why us? Why did your father take you?"

"To help with the loading. Someone he could trust. I said he was doing wrong. He'd be caught and go back to prison. It was a stupid risk. He wouldn't listen. I had to go, didn't I? I couldn't let him go alone."

"And Howie wasn't there, was he? And the warehouse was empty. It was a con game, wasn't it? How could your father have fallen for it, knowing Howie the way he did?"

"He couldn't believe Howie would do it to him. We sat out there in the dark waiting and waiting. Howie was sure to show up. Hell, hadn't he taken my father around and introduced him to the man that was going to fence the stuff? I was sick. Don's money—gone with that creep Howie."

"Maybe that was why your father filed that insurance claim. To get Gaillard his money back."

"Maybe. But that was even worse, don't you see? That was what had happened to my father. Anything for money."

"You don't know where he's gone?" Dave said.

"Maybe he told me. He was trying to talk to me, get me to forgive him. He was crying. I wouldn't listen. I was throwing my stuff in that duffel bag. All I wanted was out. He was crying outside the bathroom door while I was picking up those stupid pills. If he said, I didn't hear."

"But he was still home when you left?" Dave said. And when Lyle nodded, he said, "Report him missing as soon as you get home. Sheriff? Missing persons? It could help."

"All right, sure." Lyle looked at the door. It had opened. Trio filled the frame in her bulging jeans and striped Mexican pullover. Lyle smiled at her. She lifted her flute. It glinted in the pale, rainy light.

"Music?" she said.

7

It wasn't yet two in the afternoon, but Horseshoe Canyon was gloomy with the threat of rain when he passed the woman with the dog and swung the Triumph into the brick yard. He ached from the long, cold drive in the cramped little car back up the coast. It was stiff work getting out of the car. The woman came down the steep tilt of the drive toward him, looking worried. The dog was small and ragged and brown. Its hair fell into its eyes. The leash which it kept taut, darting this way and that, was red. Dave stretched and gave the woman a small enquiring smile.

"Mr. Brandstetter, isn't it?" she asked. He nodded, and she said, "I'm Hilda Vosper. I live just up the road." A triangle of plastic was tied over her gray hair. She wore a raincoat cinched tight at the waist. Jeans showed under the raincoat. Plastic covered her shoes. She wasn't young but she was handsome. Her blue eyes took in the front building. "Haven't you made this place attractive? Really rustic instead of just shacky the way it was before."

He didn't say he had liked it well enough the way it was before. "What can I do for you, Mrs. Vosper?"

"You're in insurance," she said, "somebody told me. I've been wondering why the checks haven't come for the mudslide damage. Did you get yours?"

"Yes. You mean you haven't received any checks?"

"The first ones, yes. But there should be others."

"All I know about insurance is death claims," Dave said. "I'm sorry. I'd like to help, but I can't."

"Yes, well, I just thought I'd ask," she said bleakly. "They don't answer letters. No one on the telephone knows anything." The dog had wrapped the leash around her legs. "Thank you," she said, turning to unwind the leash.

"Nice to meet you," Dave said.

The big wooden rear building was cold, no fire in the grate, and he kept the sheepskin coat on while he rang Salazar to tell him about Howie O'Rourke. Salazar's flu sounded worse. Dave splashed brandy into a snifter, tasted it, shed the coat, and headed for the bathroom. He cranked the Hot tap in the shower stall and, when steam began to billow out, shed his clothes. He swallowed brandy again, used the Cold tap to tame the heat of the spray, and was about to step under the spray when Cecil put his head in at the bathroom door.

"Where were you last night?" Dave said. "I phoned at midnight."

"They put me right to work." Cecil wore the big stiff white robe. He came into the steam and shut the door. "Night shift. I go in at four-thirty, get off at midnight. I was here by twelve-thirty." He dropped the robe. "No way for me to let you know, was there?" He drank some of the brandy. "Mmm-mmm! I could easily get hooked on that stuff." He raised his eyebrows and nodded at the shower.

"Are we going to get in there? Or let all that gorgeous hot water run down to the sea?"

"Come on," Dave said. It was a big enough shower. For almost anything. Almost anything was what they did. They even got clean. They rubbed each other dry with tent-size towels. Dave said, "I'd rather have you around nights. What about dinners by candlelight? What about plays and operas and ballets? Even movies? Even, God save us all, television?"

"You can applaud me"—Cecil flapped into the robe again—"on the eleven o'clock news." He opened the door, gasped, shuddered. "Shit, man, we're on a fucking ice floe. I got to put on clothes." His feet thumped on the stairs up to the loft. Dave put on his own bathrobe and followed. Rain pattered steadily now on the slope of roof just above them. Quivering with cold, Cecil whipped into undershorts, T-shirt, bulky white sweater, warm wool pants. He sat on the broad, unmade bed, to pull on thick white socks. "Maybe I won't have that shift too long. If I'm as dazzling as I think I am." He bent to tie his shoes.

"I hope you're right." Dave opened drawers and got out clothes for himself. "Damn Edwards, anyway."

"You're not thinking," Cecil said. "How many plays, operas, and ballets did you see last night? You were working, right? And the night before? Working." He jumped up from the bed and ran downstairs. "I am going to start a fire, warm this place up."

Dave dressed, listening to the rattle of kindling in the fireplace grate, the whoosh of the gas jet, the snap and crackle of green wood. He smelled the smoke. He went down the stairs. "My days begin early too," he said, and

78

stood and watched the flames curl around the sticks, hungry to grow. "Cecil, we'll almost never see each other—not this way. Forget this kept-boy nonsense, and go with me where I go and when I go, and stay with me when I stay."

Cecil had been kneeling. He got to his feet, brushed his hands, set the fire screen in place. "Let's try it for a while," he said. "For my sake. Make me feel decent, okay?" He laid his hands on Dave's shoulders and put a kiss on Dave's mouth. "I want to be with you just as much as you want to be with me." He managed a wan little smile, and a little rise of his wide, bony shoulders. "Who knows how long I can stand it? Did you think of that?"

"No, but now that you've said it, I'll probably bring it up fairly often." Dave smiled. "All right. No dinners by candlelight. How about lunches? Starting today, now."

Cecil looked at that daunting watch. "Too late. All the chairs will be up on the tables by now. Waiters shooing out the last expense-accounters." He went to the door. "What we are going to do is open cans. I've checked out your cupboards. Mrs. Snow's clam chowder, with an extra can of clams, cream, butter, white pepper." He turned at the door. "Did you find him?" He opened the door.

"He doesn't have the answer." Dave stepped out and Cecil shut the door. They trotted, heads down under the heavy drops that fell from the matted brown vine on the arbor, across to the cookshack. "If we make this quick"—Dave lifted down a deep saucepan—"you can go with me to see a man who may have the answer."

Dave had been here before, years ago, with Rod Fleming, a decorator he'd lived with for twenty years, until Rod had died of cancer. But if Dave had heard Don Gaillard's name at that time, he'd long since forgotten. The shop was not, as Lyle Westover remembered it, in a basement, but on a side street just off La Cienega. Two-story, living quarters up an outside staircase, the building was grubby white stucco. Rain made runnels in the dirt on the plate glass, through which gleamed faintly the pale curves of carved chair arms and sofa backs, awaiting stain and varnish. A mahogany table glowed dark red.

The street door stuck at the bottom and had to be kicked to make it open. There were fresh-cut wood smells inside, smells of hot animal glue, the ether smell of shellac. No one was among the unfinished pieces in the front room, but a power-saw snarled in the back of the shop, beyond a plywood partition in which a doorway showed light. And when Dave looked through the doorway, he remembered Don Gaillard's round, snub-nosed face. The hair above it had been dark and thick when he'd last seen it. Now it was gray and thin on a pink scalp. But the man still had boyishly rosy cheeks and blue eyes that were a little too gentle. He switched off the saw when he noticed Dave and Cecil, and came through a snowfall of sawdust toward them. His eyes flicked quickly over Cecil, obviously pleased with what they saw. He held out his hand. Its grip was firm.

"It's not about furniture." Dave handed over his card. "It's about Charles Westover."

"Insurance?" Gaillard looked puzzled.

Dave explained about the claim on Serenity's policy.

"Oh, no!" Gaillard was shaken and the color left his face. "Surely not. She was such a lovely little girl. Oh dear, oh dear."

80

"The insurance people aren't sure it's true," Dave said. "Charles Westover is in big financial trouble, and they think this was a try at getting a little money."

"No." Gaillard tried to look and sound firm. "Charles would never do a thing like that."

"You know he served a term in prison?" Dave asked.

Gaillard snorted. "The kind of scum involved in that case always arrange for someone else to take the punishment."

"He didn't bribe witnesses?" Dave said. "He didn't stand by while men were murdered?"

Gaillard said impatiently, "Just why are you here?"

"Westover's disappeared. I'm trying to find him. He borrowed twenty thousand dollars from you the day before he vanished. I thought you might know where he is."

A door at the back of the shop opened. Damp air came in, the rattle of rain outside on trash barrels in an alley. The rosy, snub-nosed woman who entered was in her sixties, damp scarf over her hair, old raincoat, scuffed shoes. From under her coat she took a brown paper sack. "Soup," she said. "Eat it while it's hot." She set the bag on a workbench, turned, and was startled to see Dave and Cecil. "Oh, I'm sorry," she said.

Gaillard stood as rigid as something he'd put together out of wood with pegs and glue. He didn't look at her. He didn't make introductions. Between clenched teeth, he said, "Good-bye, mother." When she had gone back into the dismal alley and pulled shut the heavy, metal-covered door after her, Gaillard glanced over his shoulder at it, then asked Dave in an indignant whisper, "Who says I lent him twenty thousand dollars?"

"Lyle," Dave said. "You remember Lyle?"

Gaillard's testiness melted in a sentimental smile. "When he and Serenity were young, we had wonderful times together—Disneyland, Sea World, *The Sound of Music.*" He shook his head fondly and laughed. His teeth needed looking after. "I loved being with those children. I guess I never grew up, myself." He sobered. "I miss them."

"They miss you," Dave said. "Lyle does. He never understood why you stopped coming around. What happened?"

Gaillard looked away. "It's not relevant."

Cecil said, "His parents found out you were gay—right?"

"What?" Gaillard grew red in the face. "What did you say?" His eyes narrowed. "How dare you come into my shop and say such things to me." He closed big fists and took a step. "Get out of here."

Cecil backed, hands up, laughing shakily. "Hey, man, it was a friendly question."

Dave caught Gaillard's arm. "Easy. Think. How would he guess that? How would I?"

Gaillard blinked, dropped his arms, stared at the two of them for a second, smiled a sickly little smile. "Oh," he said. "I see."

"But there's more, isn't there? The reason you gave Westover that money when he turned up after ten long years was that you were in love with him, and you never stopped loving him, not when he got married, not when he finally told you to go away."

"He never did!" Gaillard cried. "It was Anna—that wife of his. She was the one who forced him to stop seeing me." Tears blurred his eyes, his voice broke. "What harm were we doing her? What harm? For ten years, she never knew, and then she stumbled on us together, and her life was ruined. Ridiculous." His mouth twisted in contempt. "It had never made the slightest difference between them. She hadn't the vaguest. He was a loving husband and a wonderful provider. We saw each other alone once a week—oh, sometimes twice. She never guessed." His thick fingers wiped at his tears. He took a deep breath. "All right. He was in trouble, and I helped him. He'd have done it for me."

"You really believe that?" Dave said.

Gaillard swelled up. "Absolutely. I know him better than anyone in this world."

"Then you won't be surprised to learn what happened to the money you lent him." Dave told the story as Lyle had told it to him. Gaillard sagged a little, but he kept a straight face. No surprise showed, no disappointment. When Dave stopped talking, what showed was charity:

"Poor Chass. What rotten luck. On top of all his other troubles. And Lyle left him alone? At a time like that? I'm surprised. He always seemed so sensitive."

"He still is," Dave said. "He tried to kill himself. Luckily, there weren't enough pills."

"Kill himself!" Gaillard's hand splayed open against his big chest. "Whatever for?"

"Out of shame for how his father used you."

"But—I was happy to have the chance to help Chass. Surely Lyle must have known that."

"He knew," Dave said. "That only made his father's taking advantage of you more humiliating. Charles didn't come back here afterward and apologize, now, did he?"

"Doesn't Anna know where he is?"

"I asked her for the names of friends he might have gone to. She didn't mention yours."

Gaillard's laugh was brief and sour. "No, I imagine not." He looked straight and deliberately into Dave's eyes. "I haven't any idea where he's gone. But I'm sorry that he didn't feel he could come back to me."

"You're not sorry about the twenty thousand dollars?"

"I'm sorry that it didn't save him," Gaillard said.

"Call me if you hear from him, will you?" Dave said.

"You're mistaken if you think he tried to cheat your insurance company," Gaillard said. "He's not like that."

"He's changed," Dave said. "You didn't notice?"

"He will always be the same to me," Gaillard said.

Outside, angling their long legs into the Triumph and out of the rain, slamming the doors, Dave starting the engine, Cecil lighting cigarettes for them both, they looked at each other. Cecil passed Dave a cigarette.

"He's lying about something," he said.

Dave let the handbrake go, and rolled the little car to the corner to wait for a speeding stream of rain-glazed cars to splash past. On that long midnight drive back from El Segundo in the Rolls, had Lyle, without guessing it, actually managed to make his father see himself for what he had become? "You think Westover came back here, begging forgiveness for wasting Gaillard's money, and Gaillard smashed his skull in with a Queen Anne leg?"

"Why wasn't it his life savings?" Cecil said. "No way did he want his mama to know about it. And he was not telling us everything, man. Something he knows we aren't ever going to know, you know? And maybe that was it."

"Uncle Don." Dave jammed the stubby shift stick into

low, and the Triumph shot across La Cienega, on its way to the television studios, where Cecil had to be at work in twenty minutes. "Lyle called him 'the kindest man.' "

"He was about to saw me up on that table," Cecil said.

"Like Pearl White?" Dave said.

"Pearl?" Cecil said. "White? Will you be serious?"

But both of them were laughing too hard.

A voice said, "I thought I'd find you here."

Romano's was quiet in its aromatic shadows, white napery and candlelight. It was early for dinner. Silver and glassware glinted on empty tables. Dave had come straight here from dropping off Cecil. He would pick him up at midnight. It was going to be a long evening. He had begun killing it with double Scotches. Then there'd been a simple little salad, fresh-baked salt bread, sweet butter. Now there was *ris de veau à la crème et aux champignons,* and a bottle of Sunny Ridge *pinot blanc* 1975. He was trying to keep from feeling sorry for himself. He looked up.

Miles Edwards looked elegant in handloomed tweed. His smile was tentative. He held a manila envelope. "All right if I join you?" Dave lowered his head and went on eating. Edwards sat down. He laid the envelope beside his place setting. "I'm not here to apologize," he said.

Dave tore off a chunk of bread and buttered it. He didn't look at Edwards. "I'm pleased about you and Amanda. Delighted. I thought I'd made that clear."

"About Cecil," Edwards said. "I'm here to explain."

"If I wanted an explanation," Dave said, "I'd have asked for it. An explanation isn't going to undo the mischief you've made. Suppose we forget it."

Edwards tugged at the snowy cuffs of his linen shirt so

that they showed an inch below his jacket cuffs. "He's very young," he said.

"So are you," Dave said, "or you wouldn't be trying this." He looked around the hushed restaurant. "Where's Amanda?"

"Dining with clients. In Malibu." A waiter came in a black velvet jacket with gold trim, and Edwards asked for Wild Turkey. Conspicuous consumption, 110 proof. "I could have tagged along, but I thought we ought to have this talk."

"Some people"—Dave laid his fork in his plate and faced Edwards squarely—"don't mind being manipulated. Some are too stupid to notice. Some can't live without it. I don't like it. Don't try it again. Not now. Not ever."

"You're good at what you do," Edwards said. "You're a superstar. You didn't get that way with a closed mind. You're acting emotional. Why can't you be fair with me?"

Dave laughed, shook his head, picked up his fork again, and went to work on the creamy sweetbreads and mushrooms. He drank some of the crisp wine. He touched his mouth with his napkin and laughed again. "Emotional," he said. "Why in the world would I be emotional?"

Edwards said, "Because you love that boy, or think you do. What about him? What about his future?"

"He wants to be a death-claims investigator," Dave said. "He helped me out on a case, year before last, and decided it beat running around rainy airports shoving microphones in the faces of politicians. He still thought so, until you took it upon yourself to tell him he wouldn't be a death-claims investigator—that he'd only be a dirty old man's fancy boy." Dave picked up his fork and laid it down again. " 'Be fair'? What was fair about that?"

"It was important." Edwards's mouth tightened inside its neat frame of black beard. "It was my duty."

"Jesus." Dave sighed, picked up his fork, and ate the rest of what was on his plate. He drank wine again, and refilled his glass. "You're a prig, aren't you?" he said. "I didn't think they cropped up in your line of work."

"By 'be fair,' " Edwards said, "I meant, do me the courtesy of letting me explain. I meant, make an effort to understand. I had a reason." The waiter brought his drink and a menu and went away. Without looking at it, Edwards laid the menu on the manila envelope. "I meant, why won't you listen to me?"

"If he wasn't a male," Dave said, "we wouldn't be having this cozy chat, now, would we?" He lit a cigarette and raised a hand to bring the waiter back. The odds were awful, but he still wanted to enjoy this. He would have coffee and brandy. Maybe he would act like Trio Foley and devour one of Max's giant chocolate mousses. "If he was one of those jiggly young women you brought around—the ones who throw pies on television? You're worse than a prig—you're a bigot."

"Wrong." Edwards shook his head emphatically. "No way. Why not give your paranoia a rest for a minute and just listen to me?" He was showing anger now, and that pleased Dave. He watched the boy's sun-browned hand shake as he picked up his stubby glass and drank. "I went through what you're about to put Cecil through." He set the glass down, slid the envelope from under the menu, and pushed it at Dave. "Look inside."

Dave blinked at him, shrugged, opened the flap, and slid from the envelope eight-by-ten glossy photographs. They were of a naked young man. The top one was. He was slender, his skin was dark, his hair very long, he had no beard or mustache, but it was Miles Edwards. If nothing else showed that, those pale gray eyes did. The waiter came back and looked over Dave's shoulder. Dave glanced at Edwards, who looked pained if not panicked. Dave slid the first photograph off the stack. The second one involved Edwards with a long-haired blond boy. Naked, and at play on a beach. Not volleyball. Dave looked up at the waiter, young, stocky, his crinkly black hairline low on his forehead. His name was Avram, and he grinned.

"Don't stop now," he said.

Dave smiled and obliged, turning the photographs over slowly. Some involved two youths, some three, but all featured Edwards. In some, he was alone, but even in these he was sexually active. Dave slid the photographs back into the envelope.

"Nice prints," the waiter said. "Good lab work." Sweat moistened his upper lip. His eyes were large and dark and they pleaded with Edwards.

"Coffee, please," Dave said, "and Courvoisier."

"And you, sir?" the waiter asked Edwards.

Edwards was surly, growled, "Wild Turkey," and handed over his glass. The waiter almost dropped it. He went off, and Edwards said, "I got lost in that world. The man who took those pictures picked me up from a high-school playground. He made me feel special. I lived like a little god. Nothing I could think up he wouldn't give me, no place in the world he wouldn't take me—cars, watches, clothes, Jamaica, St. Tropez, Paris, Rome, Tokyo."

"If he could just peddle your pictures, right?"

"It didn't seem much to ask. He didn't need the money.

He had independent means. Photography was just a hobby. Or maybe not. Maybe only beautiful boys. Anyway, one night when I was asleep, a beautiful boy killed him. On the docks at Marseilles. And there I was, without even a ticket back to the States. I sold the Rolex he'd given me, the camera. I peddled my ass in New York till I nearly froze. Then it was San Francisco, and three successive cases of the clap, and getting locked out of the last ratty room I could get. Then I went back to my family. I was damned lucky they forgave me."

"I don't pick up sailors," Dave said.

"But you're going to die," Edwards said, "long before he does. You know that. What kind of lies are you telling yourself?"

"I've listened to you," Dave said. "I don't want to listen to you anymore, all right?"

Edwards stood up. "Where's the men's room?"

Dave pointed. "On the way to the kitchen."

Edwards went that way. The waiter brought Dave's coffee and brandy and Edwards's whiskey. He gazed at Edwards's empty chair as if his heart would break. Dave told him, "Forget it. He's going to marry a pretty lady."

The waiter's shoulders slumped. He went away. Dave smoked, finished his coffee, his brandy. Edwards hadn't come back. Dave checked the men's room. Empty. He pushed the kitchen swing door. He asked the tall, sunken-cheeked chef named Alex. Edwards had left by the alley door. Back at his table, Dave frowned at the manila envelope. Edwards had forgotten his pictures.

8

Perez didn't appear to have any point, unless it was the wild flowers—lupines, poppies—blue and gold, that carpeted the desert for miles around in all directions these few weeks in February. A road sliced through the town, kept minimally paved, probably for the sake of those same few weeks. Perez had a gas station for wild-flower viewers. It had what a faded signboard boasted was a DESERT MUSEUM & GIFT SHOP, where a two-headed rattlesnake could be seen, and where maps were sold of abandoned mines and ghost towns. A board structure with a high false front claimed to be an EATERY. A tired wild-flower viewer could even sleep in Perez, at the ROAD RUNNER MOTEL, six scaly stucco units, each with a weedy patch of cactus garden. VACANCY—naturally. On the bone-gray wooden side of the grocery store, the paint faded on a sign for OLD GOLD cigarettes. Wax shone on ten dented wrecks in the dirt lot of JAY'S GOOD USED CARS. The tavern was called LUCKY'S STRIKE. From at least one window of every structure in sight hung a rusty air-conditioning unit.

Dave had already seen Azrael's ranch, three sad shacks

painted blue, doors and windows lately broken out, the wind moving through them, through the littered rooms, stirring cheap Indian cotton hangings in the doorways, shifting pathetic scraps of clothing, tufts of mattress stuffing, feathers from ripped pillows across cracked linoleum. Death and desertion. Behind the buildings, in what had been a sometime attempt at a vegetable garden, the wind had begun filling in the holes from which, two weeks ago, had been dug up the rotted bodies of Azrael's pitiful young disciples. Serenity among them? Each corpse had a gap in its chest. None had a heart. At Azrael's ranch there had been nothing to see, nothing to remember. So why did Dave know that he was never going to forget it?

A pair of big, dusty motorcycles stood in front of Lucky's Strike. The place inside was cavernous and dim. Country-western music twanged from a jukebox. At the far end of the room, beyond a sleeping pool table, the riders of the motorcycles—boots, filthy Levis, scabby insignia on jacket backs—operated electronic games that knocked and beeped and winked. The barkeep—Lucky?—appeared to have been beaten about the head a good many times in the remote past. His nose and ears were crumpled, scar tissue jutted above his eyes. He set the beer Dave had asked for in front of him, blinked at Dave's P.I. license, and looked obediently at the snapshot of Serenity standing at the ranch with the blond, bearded, mad-eyed Azrael and the other smiling girls.

"I seen her with him. They wouldn't come in here: he didn't believe in booze, you know. But I seen them in town, when he come in, in that van of his, to pick up supplies for his place. Yeah, I seen her."

"The important thing," Dave said, "is when. Was she with him any time close to the end, when he killed the sheriff's men and cleared out?"

"They was friends of mine," Lucky said. "You know why they was there? Sanitation. To serve a paper. Some preacher wanted him and his girls out of there. Sex cult, he says." Lucky laughed grimly. "Worse than that, wasn't it? Only nobody knew it then. We was all on their side. Hippies, forty miles from noplace—nobody to see them but lizards and kangaroo rats. If they wanted to do it on the roof, who cared? But this preacher couldn't rest. He must have watched them through a spyglass. Claimed the place was filthy, a pigpen, not fit. Raised hell with the department of health and sanitation. County. They wrote up the paper just to get the son of a bitch off their back. And Lon and Red drove out there to serve it. Marked car, of course, uniforms, revolvers on their hip, of course. And they park the car and start for the door, and this Azrael's there with a shotgun. Didn't wait to hear what they was there for. Thought they'd found out he murdered all them girls, didn't he? Blew their heads off, just like that."

The door opened and let in sunlight for a moment, along with three youngsters swinging crash helmets—more motorcyclists? No. Two of them were girls in very short shorts, kneepads, high-top shoes, padded vests over T-shirts stenciled Sand Hoppers in a circle surrounding a drawing of a dune buggy. Lucky served them, and the squat, black-bearded youth with them, Coors in cans, which they carried along to the electronic games. Lucky returned to Dave. "I can't say for sure how long before that I seen her." He pushed the snapshot away from him. "Why do you want to know?"

"It's an old picture," Dave said. "The last her family heard from her out here was two years ago."

"That a fact?" Lucky drew the picture toward him and squinted at it again. He shook his head. "No, that's her. She was usually the one who come into Perez with him. Always wore one of them, whatyacallit, dashikis? Nothing under it. Sun in the street, you could see her naked right through it." He handed the picture to Dave. "No, I'd say no more than a month, six weeks ago." He watched Dave slide the picture into his jacket pocket. His mouth was grim. "Guess that means she was the last one he killed, don't it? Who the hell do you suppose he fed the heart to?"

Dave stared. "What did you say?"

"After he killed one, he made the other ones eat their heart. Didn't know that, did you?" He looked smug.

"Am I supposed to believe it?" Dave said.

"Lon and Red wasn't my only friends in the sheriff's office. There's this diary this Azrael left behind. They ain't saying nothing to the TV people and the newspaper writers about it. District attorney's got it under lock and key for the trial."

"Names," Dave said. "The names of the girls?"

"If they was in there, you wouldn't be here, would you? The D.A. wouldn't have kept the names back—parents all over the country wondering if that's their little girl that ran off? Nope. Come to writing about them girls, he'd draw a little flower, or a moon, or a star, or a cloud—I don't remember what-all. No names. Oh, yeah, one was a bird, too—that's it, a little drawing of a bird."

"Dear God," Dave said.

"But let one of them do anything he didn't like—talk back, disobey some crazy rule he made—he killed her, cut her heart out, roasted it, made the other ones eat it so they'd remember to do like he told them. Lot of other stuff in there, too, stuff you wouldn't believe. He was a mad dog. You know what Azrael means? Angel of death. Another beer?"

"That's enough," Dave said.

"Then it's over?" Cecil asked. "Tomorrow you write up your report, and Banner sends him his twenty-five thousand dollars?" It was one in the morning, rain on the roof. They sat watching the fire, sat on the couch under the looming rafter shadows of the big rear building, and ate wedges of warm quiche, and drank cold white wine. "Only where do they address the envelope? That's not your problem, right?"

"Tomorrow I do not write my report," Dave said.

"But now you know she was there to the end."

"Alive," Dave said. "Lucky saw her alive. Banner wants proof she's dead. They want to know that unclaimed corpse in the San Diego County coroner's refrigerator is Serenity Westover's. I can't prove that."

"Perfect teeth, perfect bones, dark hair." Cecil stood up, holding his own empty plate, and reached for Dave's. "Same size, same age. Don't you think it's her?"

"Just leave those till morning," Dave said.

Cecil looked doubtful. "Draw ants," he said.

"Too cold and wet for ants," Dave said. "Sit down." Cecil set the plates on the hearth, picked up his glass from the pine couch arm, grinned, and sat down. Dave put an arm around his bony shoulders. "I'm nearer to thinking it's her now. I was sure it wasn't when I was down there to talk to the medical examiner the other day. That's why I didn't go to Perez then, didn't even think of it. The postmark was old. These kids go to a place like that, get restless, wander off to some other place they're not going to like any better."

"Unless it's Guyana," Cecil said. "They didn't wander off from there, did they? And they didn't wander off from Azrael's ranch, either, look like. Blue paint?"

"Sky blue," Dave said.

Cecil said, "If you couldn't get proof for them, how do they think they are ever going to get it?"

"When someone catches him," Dave said.

Cecil shivered. "Would you want to catch him, touch him, even look at him? Would you want to hear what comes out of his mouth?"

"I don't want to think about it anymore today, all right?" Dave turned Cecil's face from the firelight and kissed his mouth. "What are we sitting here for? It's late. Why aren't we in bed?"

"I been wondering that, myself." Cecil tossed off the last of his wine. But halfway up the steps to the loft, Dave following him, hands on his narrow hips, Cecil stopped. "I forgot. There's a message on your answering machine. I was here. I answered the phone, but I couldn't under-stand him."

"Lyle Westover," Dave said.

"Finally, I apologized all over the place, and said why didn't he call back, and I wouldn't answer, and he could put the message on the tape, and maybe you'd under-stand it."

Dave sighed, let go Cecil's hips, and went back down the

stairs. "It could be important," he grumbled, and punched keys on the machine. He had to listen three times, but at last he puzzled out the message. Lyle was back in the house on Sandpiper Lane. Checks should have been waiting for him from the musicians' union. They weren't. The mailbox was empty except for a gas bill, new. Did Dave think Lyle's father was picking up the mail? Dave hoped so. He lifted down the sheepskin jacket from a big brass hook beside the door. He called, "I have to go out. See you for breakfast."

"What!" The bedframe jounced. Heels thumped the loft planks. Cecil scowled down at him over the railing. He was naked, the firelight glancing off his blackness. "You going out? You leaving this?" He showed Dave what he meant. "What am I supposed to do with it here all by myself all night long?"

"You can bring it with you." Dave shrugged into the coat. "If you don't mind missing your sleep."

"Sleep would not be what I missed." Cecil vanished from view. "Wait for me. I'll be right there."

Cecil's head lay on Dave's shoulder. The boy was asleep, his breathing soft, slow, regular. They sat in the Triumph on Sandpiper Lane in the dark and the cold rain that the sea wind kept catching and rattling like grains of sand against the window glass. The wind, the rain, smelled of the sea. Dave stared at the heavy-headed silhouette of the iron mailbox down the street at 171. He checked his watch. Not that there was any point to that. Westover might come for his mail at any hour, so long as darkness held. It was twenty minutes past three.

Moving carefully so as not to disturb Cecil, Dave shifted

his position an inch or two on the grudging bucket seat. Painfully he drew up one cold-stiffened leg until the knee touched the little leather-wrapped steering wheel. He straightened the other leg, the knee joint snapping. He tugged up the woolly collar of his coat and huddled down into the coat a little farther, seeking warmth. Cecil murmured but did not waken. Dave fell asleep.

What woke him he did not know, but he sat up fast and straight. Cecil mumbled "What?" and rubbed a hand down over his face. "It's him," Dave said, and with a sleep-numb hand fumbled for the key in the dash. Through the drizzled windshield he watched a figure yank open the mailbox at 171, grope inside it, shut it again, and, hunched up against the rain, scurry across the black glossy pavement to a big dark car that waited with glowing taillights.

Dave's fingers found the cold little key and twisted it. The motor stuttered, coughed, quit. Cold. Dave twisted the key again. The starter mechanism gave its singsong whine. The big car moved away up the street. The Triumph's motor caught, Dave pedaled the accelerator. The motor choked and quit again. "Shit!" Cecil's hands gripped the dash, he bounced in his seat. "Come on, baby, come on. We gonna lose him, for sure." The red lights of the big car disappeared around the bend where the lonely streetlamp glowed sallow in the rain. The Triumph's motor caught, sputtered, smoothed out. Dave pawed for the leather-covered knob of the gearshift, moved it, remembered just in time to release the handbrake, eased down on the gas pedal, and they were moving.

Dave didn't waste time with the tangle of curved streets. He headed for the beach, the coast road. At the top of a hill, they saw the big lonely car below just as it swung onto the coast road, heading north. Skidding on the curves, they followed. Dave kept distance between them. There was no traffic, nothing but occasional massive eighteen-wheelers hulking along at seventy and eighty miles an hour, their turbulence knocking the Triumph almost out of control as they roared past. Not the big dark car. It held a steady pace on a steady course.

"He doesn't know we're tailing him," Cecil said.

The harsh lights of another semi glared in Dave's eyes from the rearview mirror. He edged the Triumph to the road shoulder. The truck hurtled past, huge wheels churning loops of water over the Triumph. Muddy water. It took the wipers a moment to clear the windshield. The high, square-cornered shape of the truck with its points of warning light diminished ahead of them. Under a high black bluff, it turned from sight. But down the clear highway the dark car was nowhere to be seen.

"We lost him," Cecil said.

"He turned up a canyon," Dave said.

Yucca Canyon, it was called. The road was narrow and crooked and steep. The little wheels of the Triumph hammered in potholes. Water dashed against the underside of the car. Big rock outcrops loomed in the headlights. Old oaks bent crooked limbs over the road. They didn't sight the dark car again. Maybe this hadn't been Westover's turnoff after all. Maybe Dave had guessed wrong. If Westover had realized he was being followed, all he'd have had to do was switch off his lights for a minute and crawl, say, into the shadow of that bluff to be out of sight. Visibility was that bad. Dave was ready to turn back, but then there

98

the big car was again, a hundred yards on up the winding road, rounding a bend, yellow headlights raking brush and rock sparkling with rain. Dave pressed the gas pedal hard, and the Triumph began skidding on turns. The canyon yawned deep and dark below them, and Cecil's eyes grew big and he sat very still.

The pitch of the road turned downward, and soon they sped past a crossroads where a filling station slept, a building-supply yard behind hurricane fencing, a frame building that was a grocery store. Weak, watery night lights lit them dimly. The big car was out of sight again, but in a moment it would reappear up ahead. It had done that twenty times in ten miles. But now they drove fast and for a long time and didn't see it again. Dave pulled the Triumph up under a clump of dripping manzanita. He backed it, swung it around, and headed it down the way they'd come. At the crossroads, he took the turnoff he should have taken first. They crawled along twisting, climbing roads quick with flowing water, for half an hour, peering through the blackness. Dave braked the car again and looked at Cecil.

"Are you cold and miserable?"

Cecil nodded, cold and miserable.

"Let's go home and get warm," Dave said.

Yucca Canyon was even wilder and more empty than he had thought last night. At first, the road wound up from the coast among broad, low foothills, then entered a narrow pass, where it edged an arroyo overhung with the leafless, white, and twisting arms of big sycamores. Rain runoff plunged down the arroyo, foaming muddily, tumbling boulders with its force. As the bent road climbed, the arroyo widened, dropped below road level deeper, full of oaks, and the mountains reared higher, rockier. Sometimes the road was a narrow shelf cut into cliff faces almost straight up and down. The drop from the road edge was steep and far to the bottom. That was what Cecil had been able to see or sense last night from the passenger seat while Dave had skidded the car around these crimps of ragged blacktop, what had made him silent.

He slept now, lean, long, naked, sprawled facedown in the broad bed on the loft, warm under blankets, unaware, Dave hoped, that he was alone. Dave had kept waking up, wondering if it was time yet to come back here. At dawn he had crept quietly into clothes, shaved, fixed coffee in the cookshack and heated a Danish and eaten it. He'd put on the sheepskin coat and started the Triumph, worrying at the protests of the noisy little valves, afraid they would waken the boy. They hadn't. Now he checked the time on his wrist. Eight-thirty. He wasn't going to be too early. In fact, was he ever going to encounter human life?

It was miles before he saw the first sign of it—a shacky ranch, board buildings under massive eucalyptus trees, bark hanging in brown rags, leafage shaggy dark reds, three rough-coated horses nodding in the morning sun in a muddy paddock fenced with splintery rails. Then no more signs of life for miles. Then leaf-strewn, night-damp rooftops below road level, sets of wooden stairs leading downward from clumps of tin mailboxes. Then nothing again for miles. He wanted that crossroads. Did it really exist? Now trails began breaking off the main road. Through the trees he glimpsed here a flash of window glass in sunlight, there a chimney with a wisp of smoke rising from it. A car passed him, heading down the canyon. A rooster crowed.

And then the road dropped sharply, and he remembered that, and at the bottom of the long drop he found the fenced building-supply yard, the frame grocery store, the filling station. A wash of mud filmed the blacktop around the gas pumps and a boy in a blue coverall was washing the mud into the road with a garden hose. He had long straw-color hair and a big frontier mustache. Dave hated to sully the asphalt he'd only just purified. He ran the Triumph up beside the pumps anyway. The boy turned off the hose around a corner of the station office, then came at a bowlegged jog to see what Dave wanted. From under the long, mud-stained legs of the coverall the scuffed points of cowboy boots showed. They were worn down at the heel.

"Fill her up, please," Dave told him, and got out of the little car and stretched. The boy reached for the gas hose, said "Shit," and jogged into the office for keys. He unlocked the pump and took down the hose and stuck the nozzle into the Triumph. The pump began to whirr and ping. Dave said, "You worked here long?"

"All my life," the boy said without joy. "My old man owns it. Why?"

"Then you must know most of your customers," Dave said. "The people that live in the canyon?"

"Yeah, I guess so," the boy said. And again, "Why?"

"I'm a private investigator." Dave showed the boy the license in his wallet. "I'm looking for a man named Charles Westover."

"I don't know him." The boy pulled the nozzle out of the tank. "You didn't need much gas."

101

"Maybe I need some oil," Dave said. "Would you like to check it? And the water?"

"It's my job." The boy hung the gas hose back on the pump and worked the hood of the Triumph. "No Westover. Not unless he pays cash. Nobody pays cash for gas." He bent in under the hood, pulled out the oil stick, and wiped it with a blue rag from a hip pocket. He stuck it back in place and pulled it out again. "You don't need any oil." He replaced the stick, turned, stooped for the water hose. "You get to know their names from their credit cards. Everybody uses stinking credit cards. Country's going to hell."

"He drives a Rolls-Royce, two-tone, brown and gold," Dave said, "about fifteen years old. It's not the kind of car you'd forget."

The boy twisted off the radiator cap and fed a few jets of water in. The water overflowed. He dropped the hose, which snaked itself back across the wet tarmac and into its hole. The boy screwed the cap back on and slammed down the hood. "I remember it. Only been in one time, but I remember it. Sure."

"Westover is about forty-five, slight build, the tip of one ear is missing."

"It wasn't him." The boy wiped his hands on the rag and stuffed the rag back into its pocket. "It was a girl. Maybe a teen-ager, maybe older, twenty or so?"

"Brown eyes?" Dave's heart thumped. "Dark hair?"

"Blond," the boy said. "I couldn't see her eyes. She wore dark glasses."

Dave took the snapshot from inside the sheepskin jacket and handed it to the boy. "The girl in front?"

The boy shook his head. "Too fat," he said. "This one was skinny, sick-looking, kind of, pale." He handed back the snapshot. "Tacky, too. Ragged old sweater, dirty jeans, barefoot. I wouldn't have remembered, except what was somebody like that doing driving a Rolls?" He watched Dave put the snapshot away. "Is that Azrael?"

"That's who it is." Dave read the meter on the gas pump, dug out his wallet, handed the boy a twenty-dollar bill. "Keep the change. And tack this up somewhere, so it doesn't get lost." It was his card. "And call me if that Rolls comes in again, will you, please?"

"You think the girl in that picture is still alive?"

"It's not getting any easier." Dave got into the Triumph and rolled down the window. "You only saw it that one time?"

"Yeah." The boy read the card. "I'll call you."

"Thanks," Dave said.

Until two in the afternoon, doggedly, not missing a turn-off, he prowled the mud-slick back trails of the canyon, going slowly, searching with his eyes every foot of every crooked mile, for the Rolls—in a yard, a carport, hidden in brush. He didn't find it. He drove back down to the coast road and, with the sea glittering cold and blue in the sunlight to his right, headed home to Cecil.

9

By four o'clock, when Cecil scrambled lankily into the van to start for work, Dave standing shivering in a bathrobe in the damp, bricked yard, the sky had clouded over. The wind blew soft and damp from the southeast. It was going to rain again. Dave had promised to sleep until Cecil returned. But while Dave had been up in Yucca Canyon this morning, the telephone had wakened Cecil, half wakened him. Thelma Gaillard had left her number.

Now, at four-thirty, CLOSED hung from a grubby string inside the dirty glass pane of Gaillard's shop door, and the shop was without lights. Dave climbed the outside stairs and rapped the wooden frame of a loose screen door at the top. To the south, above rooftops, treetops, the sky was dark as a bruise, threatening. The door opened.

"Oh." She was startled. She touched her gray hair, smoothed her old brown cardigan. Her bluejeans were faded, shapeless, her tennis shoes worn. Her cheeks weren't rosy today. "I thought you'd telephone."

"I was in the neighborhood." Not true, but he liked to go, instead of phoning, to watch faces when they spoke, to look into eyes and rooms. Surprise was sometimes useful, let him see and hear what strangers weren't always meant to see or hear. "What was it you called me about?"

"Don. I don't know where he is. Come in." She unhooked the screen door and pushed it open. She glanced at the sky. He stepped inside. "Excuse how things look." She hooked the screen again, and shut the wooden door. "I'm so upset, I guess I'm just letting things go." It needed paint, but it was a neat kitchen, except for a few unwashed dishes beside the sink, an unwashed pan on a twenty-year-old stove. She led him down a narrow, dark hallway past the half-open doors of dim bedrooms, one of the beds unmade, to a living room with tired wallpaper and threadbare furniture—none of Don Gaillard's handiwork here—where a television set with bent antennae flickered and spoke. She said, "I thought you might know where he went," and moved to switch off the set.

Dave said, "Wait a minute, please."

It was a news broadcast. The pictures were of a van lying on its side in a stony ravine. The van was blue and painted with chalky-looking flowers, birds, stars, moons. The artwork was clumsy, amateurish. Men in suntan uniforms moved around the van. Desert stretched beyond. Mountains formed a ragged blue line far off. The newscaster's voiceover said ". . . definitely the vehicle known to have been driven by the missing California sex-cult guru and suspected murderer of two sheriff's deputies and at least six young women. Nevada authorities say their search will now be intensified, with—" Dave switched off the set.

"He probably wandered off out there and died," Thelma Gaillard said. "Deserts are terrible places, hot all day, freezing at night, no water. I used to worry so when Don and Chass went to the desert. Would you like some coffee? Tea?" She looked around, doubtfully. "Don may have some whiskey. It's so cold."

"I'm all right," Dave said. It wasn't cold in here. A gas heater hissed in a corner. "I'm not sure I understand. I don't know your son at all well. How would I know where he's gone?" He shed the sheepskin jacket. "How did you come to telephone me?" He sat down.

"I found your card in Don's workclothes," she said. Knitting lay on a couch that faced the television set. She sat beside it and picked it up. She only glanced at it for a second, then turned her blue eyes on Dave, but the needles began clicking in her fingers. "You see—just after you left the other day he came tearing up here in a state, changed his clothes, and rushed out. Without a word of explanation. I could see something had upset him terribly. I said, 'Tell me what's the matter,' but he just pushed me out of his way. All he said when he ran down the stairs was, 'I'll be back.' But he hasn't come back. He hasn't even called. And it's been two nights, now. And that's not like him. He never stays away nights without phoning me."

"But he does sometimes stay away?" Dave said.

"Yes, but he never breaks right into a working day, locks up the shop, runs off. He has orders to fill. He puts in sixteen hours a day down in that shop. Sometimes he won't even rest on Sunday. And why didn't he pack a suitcase? He didn't even take a shaving kit."

"He had no reason to run from me," Dave said. "Maybe somebody telephoned him."

"No. The phone up here is an extension. I always hear

the bell. No one phoned, Mr. Brandstetter. And it was right after you and that colored boy drove off that this happened. What did you say to him?"

"I came looking for Charles Westover," Dave said.

Her mouth fell open. The needles went silent. "Chass? But"—she gave a bewildered little laugh—"he hasn't seen Chass in years. Ten years, at least."

"You're wrong about that," Dave said. "Chass came to see him two weeks ago."

"Oh, no." She was positive. The needles dug into the yarn again, twisting, clicking. "You must have misunderstood. If Chass had come, Don would have brought him up here to see me. Chass was an orphan, you know. He always said I was better to him than any mother could have been." She gazed at the gray front windows, mourning a lost past, and her smile was sentimental. "I loved that boy and he loved me. He wouldn't have come without running up here to give me a hug and a kiss."

"Maybe you were out," Dave said, "at the supermarket or someplace. He came, Mrs. Gaillard. Don told me. Lyle Westover told me."

"After all this time?" She wasn't letting go her stubborn disbelief. She scoffed. "What for?"

Dave didn't want to be the one who told her about the loan. "I don't know. What I do know is that just afterward, Westover disappeared. I have to locate him. It's about an insurance claim. When I learned he and Don Gaillard were old friends, I came to ask Don if he knew where Westover was. He said he didn't."

"Don is always truthful," she said primly.

"But Westover meant a lot to him—isn't that right?"

"They were as close as any two boys I ever saw—men. After they broke up"—she quit working the needles and lifted the droop of blue knitting to study her progress— "Don wasn't the same person." She smoothed the knitting on her knees. "He's never gotten over it."

"So it's just possible, isn't it," Dave said, "that he shaded the truth to me, and went to help his friend?"

"How?" Her laugh was helpless, impatient. "I don't really understand what you're saying. Help him, how? What is this about insurance?"

"The Banner company thinks Chass may have filed a false claim. But he has worse troubles than that. Don didn't know how bad things had gotten for Chass until I came and told him."

"But if Chass isn't at home," she said, "how could Don go to him? Where?" Her look rested on Dave in mild reproach. "It was I who phoned you to find out where Don is—remember?"

"You said they used to go to the desert," Dave said.

She gave a nod and began knitting again. "They spent every weekend of their lives together, even after Chass was married. The desert, the mountains, the beach. I don't remember the names of the places, if they ever told me."

"Not Yucca Canyon?" Dave said.

Her look was blank. Plainly she'd never heard of it. "Is it so far away he couldn't get home in two days?"

"It's just up the coast." Dave stood and picked up his jacket. "What kind of car does Don drive?"

"A panel truck," she said, "dove-gray, with Don's name on the side, and 'Hand Crafted Furniture.' In yellow. Of course, it's old, and the paint's all faded now." She frowned. "What kind of troubles were these Chass had?"

Dave was back in Yucca Canyon, driving those twisty little trails, looking at cars in shrubby yards where rain sparkled on leaves in morning sunshine. No panel trucks—dove-gray or any other color. "Money troubles," he said.

"Money? Hah." Her mouth tightened at one corner. The needles clicked, bad-tempered. "Don is no fancy lawyer. You see how we live. No—if it was money, there's no way in the world Don Gaillard could help Charles Westover."

"Thank you." Dave moved to leave. "If Don comes home, will you have him phone me, please?"

"What if he doesn't come home?" She put the knitting aside, got quickly to her feet, reached out to him. "What if something's happened to him? I'm frightened." Her mouth trembled, there were tears in her eyes. "The streets get so slick in the rain. Maybe he's lying in a hospital someplace, unconscious, hurt, helpless."

"If he carried identification," Dave said, "you'd have been notified. Have you called his friends?"

She turned her eyes away uneasily. "He doesn't like me prying into his private life. He gets very angry. He has that right, I know." She sounded as if she didn't really think so. "He's a grown man, after all. But I was frantic." She looked up at Dave as if he could give her absolution. "I felt guilty even going into his room. But I went, and I found his little address book, and phoned some of them. No one's seen him. Most of them hardly seemed to know who I was talking about. Nothing but first names in that book—Pete, John, Ralph. They weren't any help."

"You don't know any of them?"

"He never brings them here," she said. "Maybe he's ashamed of me. That's how he acts, sometimes."

"I'm sure that's not true." Dave patted her shoulder. She was like a lost little girl of five who needed her tears dried. "Where's your telephone?"

She took him back to the kitchen. It was on a wall. He dialed Salazar. The deputy looking after his desk said Salazar was home with the flu. Dave doubted there was anything in Salazar's files he could refer the deputy to. He'd wanted Salazar to look for Gaillard. That might lead them both to Westover. He wasn't going to get that help. Still, the deputy surprised him. Salazar had located Howie O'Rourke. In the L.A. county jail. For breaking parole—drunk, disorderly, consorting with known criminals.

"Did he have twenty thousand dollars on him?"

"He lost it on the horses at Santa Anita."

Dave thanked the deputy and hung up. He told Thelma Gaillard, "I'm going now, but I want you to promise me something. To get on this phone as soon as I've gone and call the police, missing persons. Tell them about Don."

"Oh, no." She looked shocked. "Don hates the police. He'd never forgive me." She begged Dave with her eyes. Her cheeks were flaming red. "It's not that he's ever committed a crime. It's just little, well, indiscretions, boyish things. He gets tired and overwrought. He works so *very* hard. What harm does it do? But the police have been very nasty to him."

"He won't hate them," Dave said, "if he needs them and they help." He pulled open the door. Rain had begun to fall. The breath of the rain came cold through the screen door. "And if they find him, you let me know right away, will you? I'll appreciate it."

She stared at the phone, face pinched with dread. She

plucked nervously at her lower lip. She turned to Dave. "Isn't there anything you can do? You're a private investigator. It says so on your card."

"There's only one of me," Dave said. "There's a lot of them. Now, they'll ask you for a list of places he goes, people he sees—"

"He'd hate that," she said. "I don't know, anyway. He never tells me anything. I don't dare ask him."

"Mention Yucca Canyon to them."

"But I—" she started to protest.

"As a favor to me," Dave said, and went out and pulled the door shut after him.

He ran across the uneven bricks through the rain to the cookshack and built a double martini before he even took off his coat. While the martini chilled, he sliced tomato and avocado and laid the slices on lettuce on a plate. He tasted the martini, sighed, smiled, and switched on the radio. Brahms's *Liebeslieder* waltzes in the version for voices and piano. He sang along while he mixed a dressing of home-made mayonnaise, tarragon vinegar, sugar, Worcestershire sauce, seasoned salt. He lit the grille, tasted the martini again, and mixed a batter in a thick bowl. He dumped into the batter a half-pint of cooked shrimp that he'd stopped for on the way home from Gaillard's, spooned the batter onto the grille, pulled a slim green bottle of white wine from the refrigerator, and uncorked it. He turned over the fritters, which were a nice toasted color. He poured a tall glass of the wine and set it on the table. He transferred the fritters onto the plate, poured the dressing over the tomato and avocado, finished off the martini, set the plate on the table, and sat down to eat. But he had only swallowed a forkful of the salad, a gulp of wine, a bite of the fritters, when he remembered, and lifted down the telephone.

Lyle Westover said, "You just caught me going out the door." The syllables were mashed and jumbled, but Dave understood. "I'm flying to Nashville. A recording gig."

"I asked you to report your father missing," Dave said. "Did you do that?"

"Right away, to the sheriff, like you said. But they just wrote it down and stuck it in a file, I think. They never checked back with me. Did you find out whether it's my father who's been taking the mail?"

"It was dark, and I couldn't see him well," Dave said. "But I think so. The car was right. I'll watch for him again tonight. Look, I don't want to hold you up, but I need the answer to one question."

"I hope nobody finds out," Lyle said. "Country-western music. I'm not going to let them list my name in the album credits."

"Good thinking," Dave said. "Yucca Canyon. What would your father be doing in Yucca Canyon? Does he know someone who lives up there? Friend? Client?"

"Not that I ever heard of."

"There's an address book on his desk in the den," Dave said. "Have you got time to check through it, or will you miss your flight?"

"Trio's driving me," Lyle said, "and she goes very slowly when it rains. Rain scares her to death. She didn't get here as soon as she promised. I better go."

"Just get the address book," Dave said, "and put it in the mailbox. I'll pick it up tonight."

112

"All right. The union canceled those checks and made me out a new one so that's okay," Lyle said.

"Glad to hear it," Dave said. "When will you be back?"

"Three or four days," Lyle said, "unless something else comes up, unless I get more work."

"Good luck," Dave told him, and hung up. Now he could finish his meal. But he wasn't on the chair again before the phone rang. He sighed and lifted down the receiver. "Hello—Brandstetter."

"I'm in the Valley," Cecil said. "You wouldn't believe how wet it is out here." A siren moaned behind his voice. "I'm on this assignment. It's a hostage situation. This crazy brother is in this supermarket with thirty customers and clerks and one of those little machine guns made in Israel, and nobody knows when it will be over. One thing is clear to me. If only one reporter from channel three stays, that reporter is going to be me. So when I see you will be when I see you, right?"

"Better sooner than later," Dave said. "Try not to get shot, all right? I'll be staking out Westover's place again—unless there's a Yucca Canyon street number in his address book. Lyle's leaving his address book for me. So it looks like a late night for both of us."

"Not together," Cecil said.

"Whose fault is that?" Dave said.

"Don't start on me," Cecil said. "I'm already feeling bad enough." A voice roared through a bullhorn. Dave didn't catch the words. Cecil said, "I mean, it is going to be Noah's ark or nothing before this night is done."

"Try to keep dry," Dave said. "Thanks for calling."

"I don't think you should follow him alone."

"It's a hard rain," Dave said. "Maybe he won't show."

He finished his supper, poured another glass of wine, recorked the bottle, and stowed it away. He drank the wine while he washed the dishes and cleaned up the grille. He wanted that address book now, but he was too tired. He needed sleep. The book would be there at midnight. A few more hours wouldn't matter. He'd be a menace on the road, the way he felt. Stunned was the word for it. He ached with weariness.

He picked up the sheepskin coat, switched off the cookshack light, and ran across the courtyard to the back building, key in hand. He went through the high-raftered dark of the place without bothering to turn on a light. It was cold and damp but he couldn't be bothered to clean the grate and build a fire. He dropped the coat on a chair and climbed the stairs to the loft and the wide bed. In bed, he'd get warm. To ensure that, he kept his sweater on. He shed the rest of his clothes, slid between the sheets, and touched someone.

A voice said, "Welcome. I thought you'd never get here." A naked arm pinned him down, a naked leg. A naked body crowded against him, a mouth covered his, a bearded mouth. He jerked his head away, freed an arm, groped out in the cold for the lamp and missed. He tried to get out of bed, but arms held him. The owner of the arms was laughing. Dave's hand met the lamp and switched it on. Miles Edwards sat up in the bed, brushing hair out of his eyes and grinning. "The pictures didn't seem to do it," he said. "I decided on a personal appearance."

Dave was on his feet, kicking into his corduroys. "Get the hell out of that bed and put your clothes on."

"You're joking." Edwards threw back the sheets and blankets. He sat cross-legged. He was more beautiful now than he'd been in his teens when those pictures were taken. Still lean, but with better definition, harder. He held his hands open. "You don't want this?"

"Whether I want it or not is beside the point. You are, for Christ sake, marrying Amanda. And whether you give a damn about her or not, I do. How the hell could you imagine I'd do this to her?"

"What's Amanda got to do with it? Amanda and I are all right, we're fine. This is something separate and apart. Good God, you're old enough to know that."

"It's not a matter of age," Dave said, "it's a matter of cynicism. Obviously. But even if I did 'know that'—I don't think Amanda does know it. And I don't want her to have to learn. Not from you and me."

"She wouldn't. What would be the point? Oh, come on." Edwards got to his knees. Scoffing, but anxious. "You're not going to tell her? What for, for Christ sake?"

Dave turned away, found cigarettes on the stand under the lamp, lit one. "There's not going to be anything to tell." He leaned on the loft rail, gazing down into the dark. "We are going to forget it. And you are just very quietly going to slide out of her life, doing your best not even to leave a ripple of regret."

"Why? Because I go both ways? What do you expect me to do—change how I am? Can you?" The bed moved. Under his feet Dave felt the loft planks tremble. Edwards's arms came around him again. Edwards pressed against his back. "Come on," he pleaded. "You know you want to. I've been dying for you. I thought if you saw those pictures—"

Dave shrugged him off. "I don't think you're right in the head." Edwards's clothes lay on a chair at the far side of the bed. "If you want somebody, you don't aggravate him by everything you do." He grabbed up Edwards's briefs and held them out to him. "I haven't liked five minutes of the time I've spent with you, and I never will. Put these on, God damn it." He pushed the briefs into Edwards's hands. "And get your ass out of here. How the hell did you get in, in the first place?"

"You don't really want me to go." Edwards drew the little white knit shorts up his dark legs but not all the way. "You don't really want me to cover this up." Dave leaned on the rail and looked down into the dark again. Edwards said, "Amanda has keys, remember?"

"Jesus," Dave said. He turned. Edwards was sulkily flapping into his shirt. Dave said, "What about Cecil? I doubt that someone with your moral capacity can understand this, but what I wouldn't do to Amanda, I wouldn't do to Cecil, either."

Shaking his head in disgusted disbelief, Edwards sat on the bed and pulled on his socks. "I know how old you are," he said, "but you don't have to act like it. I never thought you would." He stood, and his glance pitied Dave. "True love?" he sneered, kicking into his pants. "Two hearts that beat as one?" He zipped up the pants, reached for his vest, his tie. "Please. That is not how human life is lived." He didn't button the vest. He draped the tie loose around his neck. He got into his jacket. "You deal with people all the time. You know that's all bullshit. People do what they want, they do what they have to." He remembered his shoes, and sat down again to put them on and tie them. "We all do."

116

"All right," Dave said. "What I have to do is throw you out of here, because what I want is not you. What I want is Cecil. And what I also want is for you not to give Amanda pain. She's had enough of that."

Edwards brushed past him without looking at him. He rattled down the stairs. Below, a ghost shape flapped white in the shadows. He'd brought a raincoat, of course. His heels tapped away. "Believe me," he shouted, "we're fine. We'll stay fine because she'll never know. Not from me." The door opened. Rain pattered outside in puddles on the bricks. "So, if you don't want her to have any pain, you just keep out of it, old man." The door slammed.

Dave went downstairs and bolted it.

10

Two steps from where Dave sat in the Triumph, a cliff dropped to the beach. He couldn't see the ocean. It was midnight and the rain still fell. But he could feel it thud against the cliff, and hear it hiss among rocks when it pulled back to strike again. The rain rustled on the car's cloth top and sifted against the glass. Charles Westover's five-by-eight address book Dave held propped open on the steering wheel. He read it by the beam of the penlight. He had passed the letter *M* and still found no mention of Yucca Canyon.

He had left the little car's parking lights on, its taillights, in case one of those juggernaut trucks decided to lay by on this patch of ground. Now headlights glared in the door mirror to his left. But what rolled up beside him was small and toy fire-engine red. A pickup truck. He had a blank second, then remembered. The door of the pickup slammed. Around its front, through the stab of its headlights, Scotty Dekker came at a jog, the rain turning his hair to taffy strings. He bent at Dave's window. Dave rolled the glass down.

"Are you all right?" Scotty shouted it so as to be heard

above the crashing of the surf. "I recognized your car." He peered. "You aren't sick or anything?"

"Just old," Dave said with a smile. He took off his glasses. "I've been reading. What have you been doing? Surfing?"

Scotty laughed, looked up at the rain. "Even I'm not that crazy. No, I've been up at my aunt's in Pismo. I'm just getting home. Good surf up there."

"That's why you didn't call to tell me about Lyle."

"Did he come back?" Scotty looked stricken. "Oh, wow. I'm sorry, Mr. Brandstetter." He wiped rain off his face with a square clean hand. "Is he all right?"

"He's all right," Dave said, "but he doesn't know what's happened to his father." He reached across to open the door on the passenger side. "If we're going to talk, you better get in out of the rain."

"I have to go. My folks were expecting me at six. They'll be worried."

"It's a bit after six," Dave said, and shut the door again. "Just one question. Did you ever hear Charles Westover mention Yucca Canyon—anybody he knew up there, any time he spent up there, anything at all?"

Scotty ran hands over his wet hair and shook his hands and made a face. "No. No, I don't think so. No, I'm pretty sure not. Yucca Canyon? What would somebody like Mr. Westover want up there? I mean, that's pretty raunchy, shacks and hippies and grow-your-own marijuana. It's all weirdos up there. Isn't it?"

"I'll take your word for it," Dave said. "Thanks, Scotty. You better go before it gets any later."

"Right." Scotty smiled, slapped the window ledge, straightened. He said, "I just wanted to be sure you were

119

okay." He bent again, blinking. "Reading? It's a funny place to read."

"It's an interesting book." Dave put his glasses on again.

"I guess so." Scotty stood erect again, looked around at the night, the windblown rain, peered in the direction of the pounding surf. He raised baffled eyebrows at Dave. Dave kept a straight face. Scotty gave a little wondering shake to his head, shrugged, said, "Okay, so long," and ran back through the headlight beams and climbed into the truck. The door slammed again. The horn beeped. The truck rolled away.

Dave grinned and went on checking addresses.

Yucca Canyon didn't appear in the book, and Dave drove back to Sandpiper Lane. The Rolls arrived earlier this morning. The rain had quit, the cloud cover was breaking up. He sighted stars through the windshield. The wind grew colder. He checked his watch. Two-ten. And the big, dark car slid past, showing nothing but its taillights. It halted at the curb in front of the dark Dekker house. The same slight man got out of it who had got out of it yesterday morning. Dave worked the lever of his door. The door opened three inches and struck the curb. He cursed. He ought to have known better than to park on the wrong side of the street. He shouted, "Charles Westover? Hold it, please."

The face that jerked in his direction was no more than a pale, featureless blur. The man turned, slipped on the wet paving, came down on one hand, one knee, regained his footing, and lunged inside the Rolls. The next second, it was on its way up the street. Dave yanked his own door shut, started the Triumph, and went after the Rolls. The big car skidded on the street bends. Over the noise of the Triumph's little engine, Dave could hear the squeal of the big tires. The Triumph hugged the curves, so that he gained on the Rolls, until it reached the straight strip of road that sloped down to the coast, when the Rolls pulled away.

It didn't stop, didn't even slow, when it reached the highway. It swung onto the highway in a wide arc, tires throwing fans of water. The turn took it clear across the far traffic lane. It looked as if it almost scraped the crash rail there. It lurched and swerved for a few seconds on the slick paving, then straightened out and settled down to gain speed. Dave checked his own meter. The needle jiggled past seventy, to seventy-five. The red taillights of the Rolls still pulled away. Dave argued the Triumph up to eighty, eighty-five. The Rolls must have been cruising at a hundred. Searching ahead for other traffic, scared that one of those giant trucks would appear, he noticed in the rearview mirror a pair of headlights behind him.

The canyon road was no good for speed, too many jogs, too many potholes, bigger tonight from the work of the new rains than they'd been last night, deeper, more of them. A good many times, the wheels of the Triumph jounced so hard in them he feared he'd break an axle. The bottom of the car scraped the paving. He was keeping the Rolls in sight, when trees, curves, thrusts of rock didn't interfere, but he judged the Rolls was going to lose him. Then he saw the headlights back of him again, and felt cold in the pit of his stomach. They were dogging him. They were following with intent. No one simply driving home would keep the speed he and the Rolls were keeping, not on roads like this, not when those roads were wet.

He wanted to get out of the way but he was on a long stretch here without the option of turnoffs, one of those places where the road had been cut into a cliff that rose sheer on the left and where the canyon yawned black and deep on the right. He risked a little more speed, but had to brake right away. There were too many bends. The lights behind him drew closer, shone harshly in the rearview mirror. For a second, he had the crazy thought that it must be Cecil. But the set of the lights was wrong for a van. Then the lights were upon him. There was a jar that snapped his head back, a crunch of metal, the shattering of glass. The Triumph leaped ahead. He pressed the throttle because there seemed nothing to do but try to get away. He didn't get away. The car following him swerved to the left, came alongside, veered into him. The lights of the Triumph streaked out over treetops shiny with rain. Dave yanked the door lever. The Triumph soared off the road. Dave threw himself into space.

"Flames like that?" Cecil said. "No way I could have missed it."

The hospital room was sunny. The wall he faced had cheerful paper on it. He had a separated shoulder, some broken ribs, and assorted cuts, scrapes, and bruises. He was groggy from drugs, so he couldn't make out the pattern of the wallpaper. Cecil's face was a blur too, but a welcome blur. The drugs had dried Dave's mouth and made it taste bad. His face was stiff, but he tried for a smile.

"It's all that Camp Fire Girl training," he said.

"Mine," Cecil said, "or yours? You hid pretty good too. No bears going to get you in that mess of brush."

"It was jump or be barbecued," Dave said.

"I didn't know," Cecil said. "Climbed down as far as I could. Muddy, sliding on my ass. No use to it. I couldn't get close. It was too hot. All I could do was stand there and cry and throw up."

"You found a phone. You got help," Dave said.

"Fire department, ambulance," Cecil said. "It was them found you. Then it was laugh and cry. I was on the ground, rolling around, howling. They had to give me a shot to get me sane. But I'm still half crazy. Shut my eyes to try to sleep, there it is down there in the dark and the wet and the trees, burning up, and you're in there."

"I'm not." Dave reached for his hand. Pain stabbed his shoulder, sharp even through the thick numbness of the drugs. Cecil's hand closed over his on the bed. Dave said, "As for the car, I was trying to figure a way to get rid of it without chagrin. So that's one problem solved."

Amanda said, "Shall I order the brown Jaguar?"

He turned in the direction of her voice. He hadn't known she was here. He hadn't known much, for how long he wasn't sure, maybe two days, maybe three. She was a trim little silhouette against a bright window. The tall silhouette beside her was Miles Edwards. Edwards didn't say anything. Amanda said, "Dave, how did it happen? You're a good driver."

"Somebody else was better," Dave said. "And meaner. Ran me off the road."

"Oh, shit," Cecil said. "Highway patrol says it was an accident. Bad curve, one of the worst in that canyon. Specially when it's wet. Talked to me about fresh skid marks, two sets. Somebody trying to pass, they said. And did I

123

know what you were doing there? I didn't say, because I wanted to talk to you first." His voice began to fade. "It was him, wasn't it? Westover? The Rolls?"

Dave shook his head against the pillows and remembered another thing that was wrong with him—concussion. His head hurt, and the movement made him feel sick at his stomach. "The Rolls was up ahead." His own voice sounded faint and far away. "It was a junk car."

"Don't go to sleep," Cecil said. "Who was driving?"

"Couldn't see," Dave said, and went to sleep.

"Sometimes you don't act quite bright," Salazar said. He sat in the neat hospital armchair and watched Dave eat bland food from a steel tray. His nose was red and peeling around the nostrils but his color was good and his eyes were clear. "We try to teach the public to give the man with the gun the money and keep your life. It's only twenty-five thousand dollars, Dave. Is Banner Life Insurance going broke if it has to pay for once? Would that be worth dying for? What is Banner Life Insurance—mother, home, and apple pie?"

"It wasn't me he was trying to kill," Dave said.

"You were the one who was there," Salazar said.

"Unhappily," Dave said. "But it doesn't make sense. I'm the man who can get him that money he's so crazy to lay his hands on. Anyway, he'd gone into hiding days before I showed up." He finished the tasteless vanilla pudding and swung the table away that held the tray. "No, he's scared of somebody else. Scared to death."

"Who's helping him?" Salazar said. "The son?"

"No." Dave explained about Lyle. "There's a skinny blond girl in the picture. Maybe. I can't figure it. A kid in a

124

gas station up the canyon says she drove in, in Westover's Rolls. Sickly-looking, dirty old clothes. But it doesn't add up. Must have been the wrong Rolls."

"Why didn't Westover pick up some hippie to while away the lonely hours?" Salazar said.

"If he did, it wouldn't be a girl," Dave said. "His ex-wife told me that. Obliquely. It didn't register until later. Anyway, no frail little girl could handle that ton of scrap metal the way it was handled. It would take a big, strong man." Suddenly he felt like smiling and he smiled. "Can I have a cigarette, please?"

"What's funny?" Salazar rose and held out his pack. The cigarettes were short and brown. He lit Dave's and his own. He eyed Dave worriedly. "Are you all right?"

"I'm fine. I think I know the answer." He told Salazar all about Gaillard's sudden disappearance.

"But it wasn't a panel truck that hit you."

"Right. And when I tried searching the back roads of that canyon for Westover's Rolls by daylight, I didn't see any panel truck. But I couldn't cover the whole canyon. Not alone. It's too big. And a lot of it is so overgrown, you can't see anything from the road. It would take a house-to-house search."

"I can't field that," Salazar said. "What reason would I give?"

"Two men missing, linked to each other by a twenty-thousand-dollar loan and an old friendship. Say, thank you for finding Howie O'Rourke. That was neat and quick."

"He's the kind who never stays out of prison long. Very bright guy. Don't ask me how he can be so stupid."

Dave said, "And a third man, linked to the first—bumped off the road and nearly killed."

"Half wilderness up there," Salazar said, "more than half. A lot of roads not even on the map. It'll be different when the board of supervisors stops squabbling about who pocketed the most payoffs from the land developers and they get their ass in gear and wangle the coastal commission into issuing waivers and permits and the rest of that shit. Civilization up there in no time. Streetlights, sewers. Wish I owned a piece of it, about ten acres. I'd turn in my badge so fast."

"They're distinctive cars," Dave said, "both of them. Easy to spot. But not by just one man alone."

"Look," Salazar said, "why wasn't it like the CHP said—slippery road, bad turn? An accident. You didn't know the car, didn't see the driver."

"It was no accident," Dave said. "It was on purpose. I know. I was there. Don't tell me it was an accident."

"All right, all right." Salazar cringed in the chair, hands up, hamming fear. "It was on purpose." He sobered. "Let me tell you about the latest wrinkle, okay? Kids with nothing to do, dropping chunks of cement on cars off freeway bridges? Driving around at night shooting down strangers on the streets? Pouring gasoline over sleeping skid-row bums and setting them on fire? For laughs, Dave, for the hell of it. We see it all the time, now. Used to be, they'd settle for showing their bare ass out the window of a car, or throwing eggs. No more. They see what happened to you on TV all the time—a guy bumps another guy off the road, and the car rolls down the slope and bursts into flame. It's a movie, right? They don't know the difference."

"Charming," Dave said. "But I don't believe in coincidences. Why wasn't it Gaillard?"

"He'd seen you, remember?" Salazar said. "He knew

126

you were the nice insurance man, maybe with a check in your pocket that would get him back those life savings of his that Howie blew on the horses."

"It was too dark for him to see my face," Dave said. "And he didn't know my car. He was protecting Westover, covering his rear."

"Only you don't know from what," Salazar said.

"Find him and ask him," Dave said. "What do I have to do—get killed before you move?"

"The department might buy that." Salazar sighed, slapped his knees, got to his feet. His topcoat lay over the foot of the bed. He picked it up. "But I wouldn't count on it." He gave a regretful smile. "Get well, all right?" He flapped into the coat and pulled open the door to the hallway. "Keep out of trouble," he said, and left.

Cheeks rosy from the cold, Max Romano waddled in. He held an attaché case flat out in front of him. Fat, beringed finger to his lips, acting conspiratorial and scared, he laid the case on Dave's bed and snapped the catches and opened the lid. The lining of the case was aluminum foil. Out of the case rose steam and wonderful smells. "Lasagna," Max whispered. "I made it myself, the way you always liked it back in the old days." He meant when the restaurant was in West L.A., with stained-glass windows and big, steel-doored pizza ovens in view of the tables, and the menu was simpler, like the rest of life.

"Sweet sausage?" Dave said.

"I didn't forget." From his bulky overcoat Max produced forks, napkins, a bottle of wine, even wineglasses. Plates came from under the lasagna. Max chuckled, setting the swivel table.

127

Amanda peered in, wide-eyed. She had on a Hans Brinker cap and jacket and kneepants, and a bulky muffler so long it nearly dragged on the floor. "Ready?" she whispered, took a last glance up and down the hallway, and slipped into the room. "Doesn't it smell lovely?"

Max had time for only a token forkful of lasagna—it made him hum, roll his eyes, and show his dimples—then was on his way back to the restaurant. But Amanda stayed to help Dave polish off the food. It was rich, and he hoped it wouldn't make him sick, but it tasted too good for him to worry about that. The wine made him pleasantly drunk. The room was softly lamplit. Cecil had left a big, battery-powered, so-called portable radio that sat on the floor in a corner and played quietly. Piano music. Schubert? When the last morsel of food was gone and the wine bottle was empty, Amanda laid bottle and plates, forks and napkins and glasses in the attaché case, and snapped the case shut.

"I'm going to rattle on my way out," she said.

"Don't hurry off," he said.

She looked at her watch. "I've got a date—sorry."

"Give me a cigarette," he said. "Sit down, and listen to me. It's important."

She frowned, but she got him a cigarette from a pocket of her Rodeo Drive boutique Dutchboy jacket. She lit the cigarette for him, handed it to him. "You always have cigarettes," she said. "Are you trying to quit?"

"Not here, I don't have them. Maybe Cecil is trying to get me to quit. I ask him to bring me cigarettes. He brings me everything else I ask for. Not cigarettes. Please. Sit down. I'm not going to like this, you're not going to like it, but I'll make it quick."

"Won't like what?" She sat on the edge of the chair. "You know I hate being late."

"Who's the date with?" Dave said. "Miles, right?"

"Yes, of course." She was impatient. "Dave, what is this?"

"It's unpleasant news about Miles," Dave said, and told her. She tried to interrupt, but he talked through her interruptions. He finished, "If you'd like to see the pictures, they're in the top drawer of my desk. Help yourself. In fact, I think it would be nice if you were the one to hand them back to him."

"Oh, stop." She stood up. "There are no pictures, and you know it. You made them up, like you made up the rest of it. What in the world is the matter with you? Did you think I don't know Miles? Did you think I'd believe just any wild lies you told me about him? Why?" She gasped a little, shocked laugh. "Good God! You're jealous, aren't you? That's what it is. Jealousy. You want me all to yourself, don't you? Or is it him you want?"

"You don't want to be saying these things," Dave said. "I'm sorry I upset you. It was clumsy, but I couldn't figure out a kinder way to handle it."

She was rigid, trembling with anger. "I've heard about malicious old aunties," she said, "but I never thought you could be like that. Not you, Dave, not you." And she burst into tears and ran from the room. She forgot the attaché case of dirty dishes. He sat waiting a few minutes for her to come back and get it. She didn't come back.

11

She was right. There were no pictures. Not anymore. Edwards had come back and taken the envelope away. Dave shut the desk drawer. He felt bad about it, but not beaten. She had good sense. When she got over her hurt, she would begin to use her brains. And they were better brains than Edwards possessed. He smiled. To smile was easier here, at home again in Horseshoe Canyon, clothed, walking around. The doctor had asked him not to leave the hospital, but he had left anyway, limping, arm in a sling, rib cage tightly bandaged, bruises colorful and tender, cuts and scrapes not yet healed. Pills of several kinds stood in little amber plastic containers on a bathroom shelf. What he needed two hands for, Cecil could help with—Cecil napping right now up in the loft. Dave sat down, picked up the phone, and punched Lovejoy's number at Banner Insurance.

"You came highly recommended," Lovejoy said, "but we didn't have in mind for you to get into it so sincerely as to get yourself killed." Dave could picture him, a sleek, well-fed black, with an easy chuckle and sad, solemn eyes. "I was by to see you, but you weren't conscious."

"Thank you for the flowers," Dave said.

"We'll cover your medical bills, the hospital."

"I appreciate that," Dave said. "Do something else for me, will you?"

"Any way I can help," Lovejoy said.

"Write Westover a letter, please. Make it read as if Banner is all cocked to pay. Say your claims investigator just needs the answers to a few simple, routine questions, so he can authorize payment of the claim. We'll have set up a meeting so he can sign the forms. Include my phone number and address, and spell my name right."

"He tried to kill you," Lovejoy objected.

"He won't, when he knows what I want," Dave said. "I should have thought of the letter as soon as I found out he was picking up his mail. I wasted time."

"You really think he'll come out to meet you? After what happened?"

"He doesn't drive all the way down out of that canyon to his mailbox every night to collect valentines. He wants that money. Don't ask me why. It's only a fraction of what he needs. But he wants it. Desperately."

"We could pay it," Lovejoy said doubtfully. "We always could have. Fifty-fifty chance the girl is dead, I suppose. I just hate not knowing, is all."

Dave told him about his talk with Lucky at Perez.

"Is a month in the ground enough for a body to rot that badly?" Lovejoy said. "In the desert?"

"Not in summer," Dave said. "But it's been winter. The wild flowers are out up there. Never seen so many. Which

131

means there has to have been a lot of rain. Which means a month may have been enough."

"I'm not going to like paying a man that tried to waste my investigator," Lovejoy said.

"He didn't know who I was," Dave said. "Anyway, you're not writing a check. You're only writing a letter. This isn't over yet. Far from it."

"I'll write the letter," Lovejoy said. "No need for you to go following him again."

"I'm not planning on it," Dave said.

He sat on a couch in the front building and ate wheat crackers that he spread with a French herb cheese, soft, white, specked with green. He washed the crackers and cheese down with bouillon from a mug. Lunch had been late. One-armed, he'd been slow in getting it ready. And proud of maneuvering it without Cecil's help. It was fancy, a kind of chicken parmesan. Cecil had liked it. They'd taken their time over it. And afterward, there'd been only just enough time for Cecil to shower and get to work. So Dave wasn't all that hungry now. The expensive stereo equipment Amanda had installed up here played the new Paris Opera recording of *Lulu* with Teresa Stratas. Berg's music made all other music sound anemic. But he disliked the way recordings hurried operas past him. He missed the intermissions. He got off the couch to turn the record over and winced. He ought to have brought the pain-killers with him. He didn't feel like hiking for them to the rear building. Maybe he ought to go back there and get into bed. It was early, but he felt bad, he ached. He stood where he was, unable to make up his mind. Out beyond the shiny black french windows, crickets sang—the pulse slow because of the cold. He switched off the stereo and, moving gingerly, made himself a drink. He returned to the couch with it and, clumsily, one-handed, wrapped up what was left of the cheese in its soft foil. He set the empty bouillon mug on the plate with the knife and the cheese. But he couldn't carry them and the drink too to the cookshack. He twitched a smile. Bad luck. He'd just have to finish the drink here and, when he got to the back building, make another to take up to bed with him. He lit a cigarette and sipped the Scotch, and the telephone rang. He could let the machine answer it. He didn't. He forced himself up and limped to the phone.

"You're looking for Charles Westover," a voice said.

"Where is he?" Dave said.

"It'll cost you." A man's voice. Oddly muffled.

Dave didn't recognize it. He said, "How much?"

"Five hundred bucks," the voice said. "Cash."

"Is this Howie O'Rourke?" Dave said. "I thought you were in jail."

There was a pause. "A dude I know went bail for me. That's why I need the five hundred. To pay him back."

"I doubt that," Dave said.

"You want Westover or not?" Another pause. Dave didn't fill it. O'Rourke went on, "Bring the money to the Santa Monica pier. I'll meet you there in an hour."

"Come here," Dave said. "I haven't got a car."

"Find one," O'Rourke said.

"A hundred when we meet," Dave said. "The rest when I've found Westover."

"I need it all up front," O'Rourke said. "You can trust me. Come on, man. I have to have the five."

"Good-bye," Dave said.

"No, wait!" O'Rourke yelped. "You've got a deal."

"It's suppertime," Dave said. "There'll be a lot of people on that pier. For the restaurants. How do I find you?"

"Just walk around out there," O'Rourke said. "I'll find you." The receiver hummed in Dave's ear. He laid it in its cradle. Why had Salazar told O'Rourke about West-over's disappearance? Why had Salazar mentioned Dave to O'Rourke? He sat on the couch, picked up the receiver again, and punched Salazar's number.

"I want to go home," Salazar said. "I'm already late."

"Howie O'Rourke just phoned me," Dave said. "He's out on bail. How does he know I'm looking for Westover?"

"He didn't hear it from me," Salazar said. "But it wasn't O'Rourke you were talking to. A man doesn't get out on bail when he's in for breaking parole."

Dave recited the conversation.

"You made a mistake," Salazar said, "giving him a name to use, saying you thought he was in jail. Whole scenario."

"What a shame," Dave said. "First mistake I ever made. But it's interesting, no? Hell of a lot more interesting than if it had been old Howie himself. He isn't truthful."

"My dinner will be interesting," Salazar said, "if I don't have to listen to my wife bitch about how late I was getting home for it."

"I'm stuck up here with no car," Dave said. "Drive me to the pier? You can arrest the man for attempted extortion and impersonating a criminal. Afterward, I'll buy you a big juicy lobster and all the booze you can drink."

"You want the Santa Monica police," Salazar said.

"I don't know anyone on the Santa Monica police. I've only got an hour. It would take that long to explain to a stranger what it's all about. Anyway, Westover's officially a missing person. His son reported it. Westover disappeared from your jurisdiction. Now's your chance to find him."

"Shit." Salazar sighed. "Okay. Where do you live?"

He peered through a grimy window in the hangar-size room where the merry-go-round used to turn, all gilt and crimson, aglitter with mosaics of mirror, the staunch and gaudy horses rising and falling on their tall brass poles in ceaseless dream. Worklights glared tonight where for years there had been only darkness. The horses lay along one side of the room, their paint and gesso stripped, their white carved wood shining softly, like the pieces of unfinished furniture in Don Gaillard's shop. Under the worklights, reaching from ladders, men painted the carousel itself. Someone was restoring it. It was going to turn and glitter again. From its bowels the orgatron would shout and wheeze and bang its drums and cymbals into the popcorn night once more. He was pleased. He had good memories of this merry-go-round. Old, very old, but still good.

He turned away and checked his watch. The man who claimed to be Howie O'Rourke was forty minutes late. Dave glanced back toward where the pier raked up to meet the palisades. Salazar leaned against a lamppost, smoking one of his little brown cigarettes. Dave wanted to go to him, find the car with him, be driven home. He wasn't in pain. He had swallowed pills to keep the pain back. But he was tired. He had walked twice to the end of the pier, along the thick, splintery planks, through pools of yellow light cast by spaced lamps along the pier, to where winches rusted now that used to raise and lower boats before the building of the marina, but where people still fished at night, elbows on chalky wooden railings, eyes on the black water below that lisped around barnacled pilings and gave back wavery reflections of the lamplight. He had been out there twice and back here to the merry-go-round barn. He was fed up. But he didn't want to leave too soon. He would give it another few minutes.

"What happened to your arm?" Lyle Westover said. He was neat, new suit, shiny shoes. A girl almost as frail as he was with him. She stood back a pace and looked shy. Her hair was honey-color. She didn't wear makeup, didn't need it. She was pretty. Poor Trio! "Are you alone? We're going to eat over there. Will you join us?"

"Thanks, but I'm working. Look, don't take anything out of your mailbox addressed to your father, all right?"

"Shall I watch for him, talk to him?"

Dave shook his head. "That would be dangerous."

"I do care about him, you know. Just because I flew off to Nashville, just because I'm going out to dinner—"

"Stop punishing yourself," Dave said. "Who's your friend? What does she play?"

Her name was Jennifer, and she played the cello.

"Dangerous?" Lyle said. "How did you hurt your arm?"

Dave told him. The boy looked ready to weep. He said, "He must be crazy. This isn't him, Mr. Brandstetter. This is not the way he is. Not the way he used to be."

Dave said, "Do you know a young woman, blond, bony, connected with your father? Someone who worked for him, maybe? A secretary?"

"Miss Halvorson was his secretary, but she was sixty. When he closed his offices, she went back to Iowa. That's where her mother lives. Her mother is ninety. I'm sorry about your arm."

"Occupational hazard," Dave said. "Don Gaillard has disappeared too. I think they may be together—up there in Yucca Canyon."

"I left the address book for you," Lyle said.

"There are no Yucca Canyon numbers in it," Dave said.

Salazar came up. Dave told him, "This is Lyle Westover. John Salazar, sheriff's office."

Lyle held out his hand and Salazar took it and hung onto it. "Are you the one who phoned?"

Lyle blinked. He said he hadn't phoned anyone. Who did Mr. Salazar mean? But his speech was thick, and Salazar didn't understand. That was clear from the dazed look he threw Dave. He let go Lyle's hand.

"I guess you weren't the one who phoned," he said.

"Good to see you," Dave said. "Have a nice supper."

Lyle mumbled and awkwardly shook Dave's hand. The girl managed a timid little smile. They went off together. Lyle walked like a badly strung marionette. He and the girl entered a shacky, gray board restaurant, where the prices were anything but shacky. Lyle hadn't wanted credit for Nashville, but apparently he'd taken the cash.

"You hustled them off fast," Salazar said. "Did I hurt his feelings? I didn't mean to. I was shocked. What's wrong with his mouth?"

"No one seems to know," Dave said. "It wasn't that. I was afraid one of you might mention O'Rourke. And when that child finds out what happened to the money his father borrowed from Gaillard, he's not going to take it well."

"Where's our man?" Salazar frowned up and down the

137

pier. "You sure there was a man?" He looked closely into Dave's eyes. "What kind of pills are you taking?"

"There was a man, all right." Dave moved off toward the shaky wooden staircase that led by crooked stages down to the parking lot below the pier. "But he never meant to meet me. Not here, not anywhere. He didn't want money. He wanted me out of my house, didn't he? Which means I'd better get back there and find out why."

"You have a blanket or something?" Salazar's suit was thin. He stood in front of the fire he had built in the grate in the back building, but it was still cold in the high, hollow, pine-walled room. Dave sat at his desk, disgustedly sorting through receipts. These had piled up from the remodeling—carpenter's bills, bills from electricians, suppliers of lumber, plaster, conduit, pipe, brick and mortar, shingles, glass, fabric, carpet. Dozens of them. He smiled. Grimly. Here were the ones he needed. Best Audio. Tape deck, cassette deck, turntable, amplifier, receiver. White's. Television sets, video recorder. Bay Office Supply. Typewriter, copying machine, telephone answerer, calculator.

"Take a blanket off the bed, up there," Dave said. "Then if you want to, you can write down these serial numbers for me." Wilshire Camera. Leica, Bausch & Lomb. He kept the receipts for the stolen stuff out, and pushed the rest, flimsy pink, yellow, blue carbon copies, back in the drawer, and shut the drawer. "But they won't turn up, will they? Exercise in futility."

Salazar came to the desk wrapped in a blanket, and made drama out of trying to keep the blanket around him while he dug out a notebook and pencil. Maybe it wasn't acting. He shivered and his nose had started to run. He hooked a foot around a chair leg and moved the chair to the desk and sat down on it. In the band of light from the desk lamp his fingers toiled, copying the numbers off the receipts.

"What you need is booze."

"What I'm going to get"—Salazar jerked his head, sniffing noisily—"is double pneumonia. This son of a bitch must have known you had all this expensive junk. Who could it be? You just remodeled. Somebody who worked here fixing the place up?"

Dave came back from the bar with brandy for Salazar and for himself. "Drink that. If it doesn't make you well, it will make you forget you're sick." He sat down again. The pain-killers were wearing off and he really did want to crawl into bed now. "Maybe you're right. But there were a lot of them, and I didn't stand around admiring what they did as they did it." He pulled the rumpled receipts out of the drawer again. "Here are all the contractors, if you want to check out the personnel."

"Gee, thanks." Salazar closed the notebook. "Okay. That gets the serial numbers of everything stolen." He drank deeply from the brandy. "Hey. You may be right about this." He closed a hand over the receipts and stuffed them into an inside jacket pocket. Blanket huddled around him, he went back to the fireplace and slowly turned in front of it, toasting himself. "Get a lot of robberies up here—housebreakings?"

"I don't know the neighbors well enough to ask," Dave said. The telephone rang. He picked it up. "Brandstetter."

"Is that you this time?" Dave didn't know the voice, not

at first. "Because I don't talk to machines. The stupid country is going to hell. No people anymore, just machines."

"You're at the filling station in Yucca Canyon," Dave said. "What's happened? The Rolls come in again?"

"Not the Rolls," the filling-station boy said, "the girl, the skinny one with the cheap blond hair. Only this time she's driving an old Impala. Right-front fender smashed. The headlight's out."

"Beautiful," Dave said. "Did you get the license number?"

"I thought you'd like that," the boy said. He gave the number. Dave said, "Just a second." And, to Salazar, "You want to write this down for me, please?" He repeated the number. Salazar wrote, the blanket slithering to his feet. The boy said, "Nevada."

"Is that so?" Dave said. And to Salazar, "Nevada."

The boy said, "You see, I didn't lose your card. I tacked it up like you said. This any help?"

"A great help," Dave said. "Thank you very much. Have you seen, by any chance, a gray panel truck, yellow lettering, name Gaillard, 'Fine Furniture' or something like that on the side?"

"Just the Impala. Green and white. Nineteen fifty-eight. The damage was new."

"If you call that damage," Dave said, "you should see the other car."

"What happened? What other car?"

"Mine," Dave said. "Up your canyon, a few nights ago, very late, in the rain, that Impala ran me off the road. I got out, but my TR is ashes."

"Jesus," the boy said. "Was it her driving?"

"I don't think so. But don't cross her, all right?"

"Shit," the boy said. "No way."

He had to be careful not to forget and roll onto his sore shoulder, and being careful of that kept him awake. He piled up pillows and read, and kept falling asleep reading. Finally he switched off the lamp. He woke startled in the dark. The diode-lighted red numerals of the clock said one-colon-two-oh. He turned cautiously to switch the lamp on again and felt something snap under his hip. The light showed him his glasses, one of the lenses popped out. Getting it back into the frame with one hand would be a neat trick. Cecil would do it. He was due. Dave frowned. Overdue. That was what had wakened him. He lit a cigarette and lay propped up in the heavy turtleneck sweater, waiting for the sound of the van jouncing into the bricked yard of the front building. Instead the sound was of the telephone. It was beginning to bore him, the telephone was. But he stubbed out the cigarette and picked up the receiver.

"You are not going to believe this," Cecil said. His voice shook. "I don't hardly believe it myself. But I am under arrest. I am at the central police division. And they are subjecting me to indignities."

Dave sat up fast and swung his feet to the floor. The boards were cold. "What in God's name for?"

"Theft. It seems I crept in and removed from your house your stereo, your TV, typewriter, camera—I don't know what-all. What I do know is that it was all of it right there in the back of my van in the parking lot outside channel three."

"I was wondering where it had gone," Dave said.

"I didn't take it," Cecil said. "I hope to Jesus you know I didn't take it."

"I know that," Dave said. He had made a bad miscalculation. He ought to have told Cecil about Miles Edwards—the photographs, the encounter in this bed, the unhappy confrontation with Amanda. "Was Miles Edwards around there tonight? The television studio?"

"He was here. Talked to me for a while at my desk. We had a cup of coffee. Why?"

"That would have been early, right?"

"Six, six-thirty. Who cares? Man, I am in *trouble.*"

"Take it easy," Dave said. "It won't last. They can't hold you if I don't press charges. I can't come, but I'll send my lawyer. He'll have you out in no time."

"How did that shit get in my truck?" Cecil said. "Who told them it was there?"

"Edwards," Dave said. "Was he around there later?"

"Later I was out in a channel-three car. That's how they think I'm guilty. Nobody at the station saw me from seven till ten. Got a call to talk to a man about a story I've been working up. On street gangs."

"Only you couldn't find the man," Dave said.

"You got it. But it sounded so good, I hung around. Then when he didn't show, I went looking for him, places I knew he went. I wasted three hours. Never did find him."

"Had you told Edwards about this street-gang story?" Dave said. "Over your friendly cup of coffee?"

"How did you know?" That was spoken to Dave. His next remark was to someone else. "Keep away from me, man."

"Down there at the glass house," Dave said, "were your keys in your pockets when they told you to empty them?"

"Told me to unlock the van first. Yeah, I had my keys."

"Then Edwards did come back and returned the keys to your jacket pocket, which he'd lifted them from earlier."

"You mean he drove my van up to Horseshoe Canyon and loaded it up with your stuff while I was out chasing around after nobody?"

"He's clever with the telephone," Dave said. "He got me out of here in exactly the same way. Listen, we're wasting time. Let me phone Abe. He'll have you out of there in an hour. Meantime, try not to hit anybody, all right?"

"An hour! I said get away from me, man. This call is my *right*. Leave me *alone!* Can't he make it fifteen minutes? I will never get the stink of this place off me."

"I'll tell him to hurry," Dave said. "And I want you to know how sorry I am. I was the cause of this, and I'm not going to get over it."

"Why would Edwards—?" But something happened to the connection. Dave thumbed the break button on his own instrument and then punched Abe Greenglass's home number.

12

Amanda said, "What in the world is this?" She stood at the door to the rear building blinking in the light that came out. She wore corduroy jeans and two layers of sweaters and a stocking cap. She wore fleece-lined boots. "I thought you'd had a stroke or something."

"Come in." Dave backed into the room and shut the door when she was inside. "I only said it was an emergency. It's an emergency. What do you want, coffee or a drink?"

"I want an explanation," she said. "Dave, it is three o'clock in the morning."

"I know what time it is." Dave went down the room under the high rafter shadows to the bar. He poured whiskey for them both. "Sit down," he called. "I don't know how soon this will be over. You might as well sit." She unwound her muffler and sat on the couch facing the fire. Building the fire, he had hurt the shoulder. The pain had been sharp and he had fainted for a minute. He felt all right now—angry but all right. He handed her a glass and

144

went back for his own. "We are going to keep a vigil, you and I. For Cecil. I want you to be here when he is delivered out of the hands of his enemies."

"What are you talking about?" She was angry too.

Dave told her. Again without permitting her to interrupt, though she tried. He finished like this: "You told Miles what I'd said to you, about the pictures, about his trying to get into bed with me, didn't you?"

"That's how it is between us," she said sharply. "We don't keep secrets from each other. Of course, I told him. It was so ridiculous. So is this. Even more so. What do you know about Cecil?"

"More than you know about Miles," Dave said.

"What?" She laughed. There was no humor in the laugh.

"Did he show you the photographs?"

"How could he? They don't exist."

"Ask Avram, the waiter at Max's," Dave said. "He'll tell you they exist. Miles wasn't with you tonight, was he? So how do you know where he was, what he was up to?"

"I don't, but I'll believe him when he tells me."

"He warned me not to tell you about our little encounter up there"—Dave jerked his head to indicate the loft—"but he didn't say what he'd do if I told you. I might have guessed he'd do something meanspirited. He's reckless, Amanda. Doesn't give a damn for anybody."

"He got Cecil a wonderful job," she cried. "And look how Cecil has repaid that kindness."

"He got Cecil that job to get Cecil out of the way here, so he could take Cecil's place in my bed. Not my affections. He doesn't know anything about affections, he thinks affections are contemptible. Don't marry him, Amanda."

She hurled her glass into the fire. She stood up. "I will marry. Whom. I. Please." Her voice was tight with rage. She turned and marched toward the door. It opened before she reached it. Cecil stood there in his corduroy car coat, looking stunned. "You—!" Amanda shrilled at him, "you—!" And she pushed him. Hard. In the chest. He was a head taller, but she caught him by surprise. He sat down on the bricks. Abe Greenglass was a few paces behind him. Amanda in the dark bumped hard against him, spinning him around, sending his attaché case flying. He was a small, thin man. Amanda stalked away across the court-yard. The black shadow of the old oak swallowed her up.

"Shee-it." Cecil got to his feet, brushing his narrow little butt with his hands. He looked at Dave, big-eyed, ag-grieved. " 'Welcome home, baby, I love you.' What's the matter with her?"

"Edwards," Dave said. "Edwards is what is the matter with us all." He went to Cecil, hugged him with his good arm, put a kiss on his mouth. "Welcome home, baby, I love you."

Abe Greenglass picked up his case, and gently cleared his throat. "You want to go after this Edwards character?" His voice was like a whisper of dry leaves.

"Come in, Abe. And thank you. Very much." The lawyer came in. Dave took his homburg and hung it on one of the big brass hooks. He helped him out of his black overcoat with the astrakhan collar, and hung that up too. "We all need a drink." He limped down the room to the bar. His shoulder yelled with pain. His hip felt as if it were grinding in its socket. "Take a seat in front of the fire, there. Get warm."

"I have to be in court early," Greenglass said, but he sat,

leaned toward the blaze, rubbed his fine-boned hands. "What do you want me to do about Edwards?"

"He's vicious, but he's not stupid." In the shadows beneath the loft overhang, Dave fumbled one-handed with whiskey, ice, glasses. "His fingerprints won't be on the evidence, they won't be in the van. He'll have witnesses to account for his whereabouts. He disguised his voice on the phone and I didn't record it, so there's no hope of a voice print. Going after him would be a waste of your time."

"What about the waste of my time," Cecil said, "in that stinking jail?" His voice shook. He headed for the bathroom, yanking out of his coat, slamming it down on the bottom steps. The bathroom light glared. Water splashed. He gargled angrily, spat angrily, angrily blew his nose. "Never get rid of the stink." He stood in the bright doorway, scrubbing his mouth on a towel. "Redneck fools. If I stole stuff, would I steal it from where I live? Would I go to work with it in my car?" He flung the towel away, snapped off the bathroom light, went to Dave. "Here, let me do that." But the drinks were ready. He picked up two of the glasses and went with them to the couch, the fire, Greenglass. "That man wrecked me. Held me up to public ridicule." He handed the lawyer a glass. "Those people I been working with. You think they were going to let this thing go past? They were out there with cameras and microphones so fast. Right on their doorstep, right in their parking lot? No way do I escape getting on the news in the morning."

"I'll stop it," Greenglass said. "What's the channel?"

"Three," Cecil said. "I'll never get a job in television again."

Dave came into the firelight and dropped onto the

couch. "You didn't want a job in television," he said. "Edwards wanted it for you."

"All right, but I didn't want it to end this way."

"Don't worry," Greenglass said gently. "I'll put a lid on it."

"Put a lid on Edwards too," Cecil said. "Put him in the garbage can and put a lid on him. He's a lawyer. He can't do things like this and still be a lawyer, can he? Stealing, framing somebody? Don't lawyers get disbarred for that?"

"Not if it can't be proved," Dave said.

Cecil stood between him and the fire. He stared. "Aren't you even going to try to prove it? You mean he's too smart for you? You never lose. How come you're willing to lose when it comes to this? After what he did to me?"

"I haven't lost." Dave looked up at him. "I've won. We've won. He wanted to separate us. He used the television job to set that in motion. And it worked, didn't it?" He waited. Grudgingly, Cecil mumbled that he guessed it had worked. Dave said, "And then he moved in to try to take your place." He explained how Edwards had done that.

Cecil squinted. "What! Why didn't you tell me?"

"It didn't mean anything. I didn't want you upset."

"Better upset than arrested," Cecil wailed.

"Right. I know that now. Doesn't help, does it? I'm sorry, and if you can't forgive me, I won't blame you. And Edwards will have won, after all."

"Ah, shit." Cecil sat down on the raised hearth. He glowered into his drink. "You couldn't know what he'd do. Wasn't me he wanted to hurt, anyway—it was you."

"I should have been gentler, rejecting him. Maybe it never happened to him before. Unhappily, what he assumed I was willing to do to you and Amanda for the pleasure of his naked company made me lose my temper."

"It wasn't that," Cecil said. "You told Amanda, didn't you? After he warned you not to."

"She was going to marry him," Dave said.

"And she still is, isn't she?" Cecil's smile was grim. "You had her here tonight to show her what an alligator he is, and it didn't work, did it?"

"Nothing seems to be working," Dave said bleakly.

"Speaking of working," Abe Greenglass said, "I want to get the name of channel three's attorney. We should talk right away." He set his glass on the couch arm and went for his coat and hat. "They won't want to show that film when they understand it was all a mistake."

Dave raised his eyebrows at Cecil. "All right?"

"Thank you, Mr. Greenglass." Cecil sighed and got up from the hearth. "But you sure there isn't some way for Edwards to be down in that jail like I was? Just for a few hours? Just to have to breathe that smell? Just to have them treat him like he was nothing, something to step on and smear into the cement?"

"I'll give it serious thought," Greenglass said. He was a ceremonious man. He shook their hands. He waited until he was outside in the cold night and the dark to put on his hat.

They slept the day away. For Cecil it wasn't easy. He kept moaning, waking, shifting position in the wide bed beside Dave. He twitched, kicked, talked. The talk sounded angry though the words were never clear. For a while, he lay sprawled on his back, and when he did that he snored. When the snores got loud enough, they woke him, and he mumbled and shifted position again. About dawn, he shouted and struck out. His flung fist caught Dave in the ribs and reminded him that they were still tender. Dave shook Cecil, woke him, and Cecil clung to him and wept. But when daylight came, exhaustion finally took the boy and, lying on his face, limp as the dead, he slept. Which allowed Dave to sleep.

Dave crept from the bed at two-thirty, showered awkwardly, clutching the hurt arm against himself, trying not to move it, which was tricky without the sling. He got into fresh clothes, which was even trickier. He went to the cookshack and set slowly and carefully about fixing a casserole. When it was in the oven, he poured a mug of coffee and started with it for the back building, meaning to waken Cecil gently, give him a space of time before eating. He was stopped, crossing the bricks under the arbor where the tips of new green leaves were showing on the dry, brown vine, stopped by a loud, painful scrape of metal out on the road. He set the mug on the bench under the live-oak and went to see what had made the sound.

It was the Jaguar from the Beverly Hills showroom. In all the excitement—if that was the right word for it—he had forgotten that delivery had been promised for today. From the hospital he'd had his accountant draw a certified check that Cecil had taken to the dealer. A white-haired black in a crisp brown jumpsuit with the dealer's name stitched across its back bent to unfasten from the rear bumper of the car a three-wheeled motorcycle. He dropped the chain into the carrier of the motorcycle, dropped the lid, and saw Dave. His face lit up as if they'd discovered each other in some hostile alien land after a long, forced separation. Dave had never seen him before. He came forward, pulling a fold of papers from a breast pocket.

"Mr. Brandstetter? Good to see you, sir. Brought your car. Beautiful." He held the papers out for Dave to take, who took them. The man in the jumpsuit said, suddenly very serious, "But you going to have to do something about that driveway, otherwise you going to rip her guts out and that would be a shame."

Clumsily Dave flattened the papers against the doors of Cecil's van. "Do I sign these?" The man in the jumpsuit found a pen and marked an X on the top sheet. "Right there, please. Here, let me hold them for you. Shame about your accident. Pretty little car. Sound like you was lucky. Burned up, Mr. Lowe say." He held the papers while Dave signed them. He put the pen away, handed Dave the white copy of the papers, folded the colored copies into his pocket, and the big loving smile was back as he laid the keys to the Jaguar in Dave's hand. "I hope you have better luck with this one." He stroked the Jaguar's sleek brown-gold finish as he passed it. He straddled the motorcycle, kicked the motor softly to life. It was very quiet, as befitted a motorcycle delivering thirty-thousand-dollar automobiles from Beverly Hills. "Anything you want to know about the car is in the manual. It's in the glove com-part-ment." He separated the syllables carefully. "Have any trouble, just call us."

"Thank you," Dave said. "And don't have bad dreams about the driveway. I'll get it fixed right away."

"This is good." Cecil mopped his plate with french bread. "Wonderful. But you could hurt yourself here. You know where the most accidents happen at home? In the kitchen. And you only have one arm."

"You needed your sleep," Dave said, and drank wine.

"Sleep like I had," Cecil said grimly, "nobody needs. I'm sorry about that. Kept you awake, didn't I? Acted like a little child can't wipe his own nose."

"My fault," Dave said. "Don't you apologize. I just hope the nightmares go away soon. None of it would have happened if I'd told you what Edwards was doing. I weighed telling you. I didn't because I thought it would spoil the job for you, and you were liking the job, you were proud of it. I didn't want you thinking you didn't deserve the job."

"I wouldn't think that. Doesn't matter why he did it. I was fine on the job." He looked gloomy. "But I'm not going back there. The way those people acted—black, white, brown, all of them. Nobody is anything to them except a newsbeat. Don't bleed in the barnyard, you know? Other chickens will peck you to death."

"Try not to think about it," Dave said.

Cecil took the empty plates to the sink. "I wish you'd think of how to put that bastard in jail."

"Come on," Dave said, and rose. "I've got something to show you that will cheer you up." He left the cookshack and Cecil came trailing after him, frowning, hands shoved deep in pockets, gait slow and moody and without bounce. But he brightened when he saw the Jaguar. He walked around it, wide-eyed, awed. His mouth shaped a voiceless oh.

"Shee-it!" He grinned at Dave, grinned at the car. "Look at *that!* Whoo-ee!" He opened the door with great gentleness and respect. His hands moved over the seats, the dashboard. "Real wood," he whispered, "real leather." He shut his eyes and breathed in deeply, wrinkling his nose. "And doesn't it smell beautiful." He pulled out of the car, faced Dave, eyes begging. "You can't drive. Not with one arm. Can I drive? Can we go for a ride?"

"I thought you'd never ask," Dave said.

They drove a long way up the canyon and around back streets. It was sunset when they reached the upper end of Horseshoe Trail. The engine of the Jaguar made hardly a sound. Its ride was smooth and easy. Remembering the jouncy little Triumph, Dave smiled contentment.

"Don't you go chasing Westover in this car," Cecil said. "Don't care how comfortable a coffin it would make."

"I'm letting him come to me," Dave said, and told Cecil about Lovejoy and the letter.

"He won't come," Cecil said. "But if he does, you make sure I am with you. Up on the loft, hiding, with a gun pointed at his head."

"What gun? You know I won't have guns around."

"Wasn't a gun almost killed you," Cecil said. "It was a car. I nearly pass out every time I think about it."

"It was a 1958 green-and-white Impala," Dave said, and told him about the gas-station boy's call.

"What is going on with Charles Westover?" Cecil said.

Dave said, "Wait a minute. Slow down. Stop."

Horseshoe Trail had no sidewalks, no curbs, only a shallow cement ditch to carry off rainwater. A brown-and-white sheriff's car, a row of red, yellow, white lights across its roof, was empty and still, with one front wheel in the ditch, beside a mailbox and a driveway that meant that back in the trees and brush a house was concealed. The name on the mailbox was Vosper. Cecil halted the Jaguar, and Dave climbed out of it.

"What's going on?" Cecil said.

"I forgot to tell Salazar." Dave limped up the driveway, which was carpeted in pine needles. The house, screened by dark deodars and lop-limbed cedars, was sided in raw shingles, like his own house, but was newer and two-storied. Cecil came running up behind Dave. The little shaggy brown dog came yapping toward him from the house. In the doorway of the house stood Hilda Vosper, talking to a young man in a tan sheriff's uniform. The dog hopped at Dave, happy, ears flapping like fur butterfly wings. Dave bent and ruffled the ears. The dog ran in a circle of delight, barking.

"Why, Mr. Brandstetter," Hilda Vosper called. "We were just talking about you. You had a robbery."

The deputy held out his hand. "Hopkins," he said. Dave shook Hopkins's hand. The little dog was facing Hopkins, barking up at him, and kicking its furry hind paws. Hopkins crouched to play with the dog. He looked up at Dave. "You've got a witness here. Always talk to people with dogs. Have to walk a dog. See what's going on in the neighborhood."

"What was going on?" Dave stared at Hilda Vosper. She wore a checked flannel shirt, black-and-white, and warm-looking gray flannel slacks. "What did you see?"

"I didn't realize what I was seeing." She gave a little apologetic laugh. "A young man, tall and slim." She smiled at Cecil. "I thought it was you. It was your van. The doors were open. Television sets, loudspeakers, all that kind of thing, were stacked up in the yard, and he was loading them into the van."

"It wasn't me," Cecil said.

"Yes, I realize that now. But it was after dark. It must have been seven o'clock. I only saw him against the lighted windows of the house. But you don't have a beard and mustache."

"Also, I am not white," Cecil said.

"But it was your van, wasn't it?" she asked anxiously.

"Stolen," Cecil said. "To get me into trouble."

Hopkins got to his feet. "Description mean anything to you?" he asked Cecil.

Cecil opened his mouth to answer but Dave interrupted. He asked Hilda Vosper, "Do you think you could identify the man if you saw him again?"

"I thought it was this young man just moving some things out of the house," she said. "But yes, I believe I could. I think I'd recognize him. Now that I see you," she said to Cecil, "there isn't much resemblance. You're stronger, your shoulders are broader. I remember thinking that he was wearing very beautiful clothes to be doing heavy work in. Of course"—she gave a little embarrassed laugh—"I didn't stare. I just glanced into the yard and passed right on down the trail. Teddy was off the leash, and he'd run after a gopher or a mole or something. I thought he might have dashed down into your yard."

"You take in a lot at a glance," Hopkins said.

"I paint a little," she said. "It teaches you to see."

Hopkins looked at Cecil. "You know who it was, don't you? You know too, Mr. Brandstetter."

Dave let Cecil tell Hopkins who it was. Cecil would get satisfaction from it. Cecil said, "He's a lawyer. His name is Miles Edwards. But you won't find the stuff he stole when you find him. I've got it back."

Hopkins looked puzzled. "What was it—some kind of practical joke?"

"Do you see me laughing?" Cecil said.

13

It came on to rain in the night. In the morning, they inched in Cecil's van along shimmering freeways clogged with cars and trucks. Over the glass towers of downtown Los Angeles, the sky was slate-gray. The rain fell softly but with no hint of ever quitting. They spent the day in noisy offices, jostling corridors, elevators, dark lineup rooms, overheated courtrooms, with assorted police officers, clerks, bailiffs, judges. With Abe Greenglass. With Deputy Hopkins and Hilda Vosper for a little while and, for a little while, with a young woman camera operator who had seen Miles Edwards drop something into Cecil's hanging jacket at the television studio. With Miles, unshaven, pale, sullen. And with Miles's father, a sick and shrunken-looking man who moved like an invalid and was acting as Miles's attorney.

The hours dragged. There was more waiting than anything else. Standing around on marble floors tired Dave and made his bruises and torn ligaments ache. Now and then he studied Cecil, waiting for the boy's exhilaration to wear off, waiting for him to get bored with making Miles suffer. But mostly his thoughts strayed. At first to Amanda, and what learning the truth about Miles was going to do to

156

her. Then to the Westover matter, sorting through all the places he'd been, all the people he'd talked to, all the words they'd said to him. Late in the afternoon, when the courts began emptying out and the plaintiffs and defendants and lawyers with briefcases pushed in herds out the tall doors into the rain and the darkening day, he found a pay phone not in use and rang Salazar.

"The Nevada plates are stolen," Salazar said. "They don't belong to any 1958 Impala. They come off a Toyota pickup in a town called Beatty—Amargosa desert."

"Is that a fact?" Dave said. "Listen, thank you for finding a witness to my burglary."

"Any time," Salazar said. "When do I get that lobster?"

"I'm going to spend a couple of days in bed," Dave said. "The doctor was right. I should have stayed in the hospital. I'm not healing as fast as I used to." Of course he'd get out of bed if Westover came from hiding in response to the letter. "I'll call you next week."

"Take it easy," Salazar said.

Cecil was beside Dave when he hung up the phone. He said, "You want to drop the charges now? Forgive and forget?" He looked a little wan.

"Had your fun?" Dave said.

"It wasn't as much fun as I hoped," Cecil said. "Tell the truth, I'm a little sick about it. A little ashamed."

"I thought you would be," Dave said. "Who do we see?"

"Down here," Abe Greenglass said, and led the way.

Dave sat propped by pillows in the bed on the loft. He had doped himself when they got home from dinner at Max's last night, and had slept from eight until noon. Cecil had brought him breakfast in bed—coffee, fresh orange juice, pancakes, and sausage, the plates covered by foil to keep the heat in and the rain off. The rain whispered on the shingles overhead, but the loft was warm, fire crackling in the grate below.

"While you were fixing breakfast," Dave said, "I tried to telephone Jay's Good Used Cars in Perez. Jay doesn't answer his phone. No one answers for him. On a hunch, having viewed Jay's operation, I tried Lucky's Strike. I thought Jay might be drinking his lunch. He wasn't. Lucky gave me Jay's home number. Jay is not at home."

"You want me to drive down and find him?" Cecil rose with his empty plate and took Dave's. "What do I ask him when I find him?" He started for the stairs and turned back. "If he sold a used green-and-white Impala?"

"To Serenity Westover." Dave nodded. "On the day Akriel shot the deputies and ran. Show him her picture. That car is just the kind old Jay specializes in."

Cecil blinked. His jaw was a little slack. "You mean you think the skinny blond girl the gas-station kid told you about is her? She's alive? She's with her father?"

"Watch the commercials," Dave said. "A girl can have hair any color she likes. A girl can lose weight any time she likes. Just pop a little pill."

"Or live under a lot of stress," Cecil said. "Only what about the Nevada license plates? Stolen in Nevada, didn't you say?"

Dave shrugged and was pleasantly surprised: this morning his shoulder hardly hurt at all. "Maybe she was trying to catch up with Azrael, had some reason to know he'd make for Nevada. That's where his van ended up."

"I know that." Cecil made a face. "But why would she want to catch up with him? I sure as hell wouldn't."

158

"Why would she stay with him for years? She was at that ranch with him while he murdered six girls—remember?"

Cecil blew out a long breath. He gave his head a shake. He went on down the stairs with the plates. Dave heard him dump another chunk of pine log on the fire and set the screen back, heard him walk down the room to the outside door. Cecil called, "This is weird. This has got to be the weirdest mess on record. No wonder you almost got killed." The door opened to the sound of rain and closed.

When he returned, bearing a fresh mug of hot coffee for Dave, he was frowning to himself. He shrugged into the corduroy car coat and fastened the pegs, put on his leather cap and driving gloves. He bent and kissed Dave, tasting of sweet, creamy coffee. He stood looking down at Dave, forehead creased. "What if Westover comes? I don't like leaving you alone, not all battered-up like you are. How can you defend yourself if he turns mean?"

"All he wants is money," Dave said.

"What if his crazy daughter comes with him? Who knows what she wants?"

"She's supposed to be dead, remember? She won't come. That would spoil their plans." He worked up what he hoped was a reassuring smile. "Stop worrying. Nothing's going to happen to me. Don't forget to take her picture. It's in the top left drawer of the desk. And concentrate on your driving, all right? Don't speed trying to get back here."

Cecil looked doubtful, but he went down the stairs again. Before he left, he called, "I'll phone you, soon as I find old Jay. I'm locking the door."

It didn't stay locked. Cecil hadn't been gone ten minutes when Dave heard footsteps cross the brick courtyard and the tinkle of keys. He reached for his pants. The door opened. With the falling of the rain on the bricks for a background, Amanda called, "Dave?" sounding a little timid.

"Ho," he said. "Warm yourself at the fire. I'll be right there. Help yourself to a drink." Getting the trousers on one-handed took time. He went down the stairs. She stood in front of the fire in knickers, boots, a fur hat, and the long, long muffler. She smiled and held out a glass to him with Scotch in it and ice. Her smile was sheepish. "I'd like you to forgive me, if you can."

"For what? Making a mistake?" He took the glass. "Thank you." He drank from the glass. "Don't brood about it. How were you supposed to know what he was? He didn't tell you—right?"

"I mean for the names I called you," she said, "for the awful things I said to you."

"What's important," he said, "is that you're all right. You're going to be all right, aren't you?"

She looked into her glass. She sat on the couch. She looked at the burning logs. "After while," she said. "Not right away." She looked at Dave. "He admitted it all to me, everything you'd said."

"That's nice. We won't have to ask Avram," Dave said. "I think he'd be a little embarrassed, telling you about those pictures."

"Miles thought if he confessed and said he was sorry, we could go right on." She gave a little humorless laugh, a little shake of her head. "I've just come from him. And, do you know, I was tempted. That's why I came flying to you. I know he's rotten, but he is so damned beautiful, Dave."

"He thinks so," Dave said. "You'll get over it."

She took a sip of her drink, rummaged cigarettes from her shoulder bag, held the pack up to Dave. He took a cigarette, she took one. Dave lit them both. She dropped the long red pack back into the bag and frowned up at Dave through smoke. "Women sometimes make a go of it with—with someone like Miles. Someone sexually like Miles."

"Not someone ethically like Miles," Dave said. "Sure, some women do. So I've read. I've never met one. I've met one lately that didn't make a go of it." He stopped talking. "My God," he said, "how stupid I am." He set his drink on the hearth and went for his jacket. "You're going to have to excuse me. I have to see that woman."

"You got the Jaguar," she said.

"Lock up, will you?" he said, and opened the door.

Rain dripped off the jungle gym whose red paint small hands had worn down in places to the dull steel tubing, rain glazed the yellow-and-blue crawl barrels, splashed in the gaudy little cars of the choochoo that never moved, wept off the steel steps of the slide, slithered down the shiny chute of the slide, and made a deep puddle at the foot of the chute. Rain pooled in the canvas-sling seats of the chain-hung swings. The low end of the gingham-print seesaw drowned in a puddle. It looked sad. But the wide windows of the playschool glowed and were pasted with cutout paper daffodils. Dave worked the latch of the gate in the chain link fence and crossed the yard. Halfway to the door, music met him, noise, the rattle of toy drums and tin xylophones and tambourines, the high-pitched piping of small voices. He looked through the streaming glass of the door. They sat in a circle on their little red chairs and played and sang and kept time by clapping their hands and stamping their feet. If he knocked he wouldn't be heard. He turned the cold, wet knob, pushed the door open, and put his head inside. The air was warm, moist, and smelled of little kids, graham crackers, banana peels, toilet accidents. He stepped inside and closed the door. The kids paid him no attention, nor did the massive moon-faced black woman in the gay patchwork smock, but Anna Westover got up swiftly and came to him, looking alarmed.

"Serenity? Have you found her?"

"It's possible. But not to talk to."

"What do you mean? What's happened?"

"Nothing lately," Dave said. "But about ten years ago something happened, and I'd like you to tell me about it."

The kids were too loud for her to hear him. She lifted her hand to indicate that he was to follow her. They skirted the circle of little red chairs, stepping over spilled toys and storybooks and stuffed animals. She opened a door and waited for him to go through, came in after him, shut the door. It was not a big office, and it was crowded with supplies—construction paper, jars of white paste, bottles of poster paint. Shelves sagged. There were boxes of wax crayons, of chalk, of small scissors, cheap paintbrushes. Cartons were stacked hip-deep—modeling clay, newsprint for painting. The desk was barely visible. She lifted an armload of stuff off a molded plastic chair with spindly steel legs for him to sit on. She sat behind the desk. The door was flimsy, the kids still loud, but it was just possible to talk.

162

"Ten years ago," Dave said, "you caught your husband and Don Gaillard involved in a homosexual act—isn't that so?" He didn't wait for her to answer. "They'd had a long friendship, relationship, and it came to an end suddenly then and there. This was why you told me that there wouldn't be another woman in his life, wasn't it? Because you were the only woman he'd ever been physically interested in. Gaillard had been willing to share him with you, but you weren't having that, were you?"

She had turned white. "Where did you hear this?"

"I pieced it together. You began it. Lyle told me how much he'd liked Gaillard when he was small, how close the friendship was between Gaillard and his father, how puzzled he was when it suddenly stopped."

"Close!" Her mouth twisted in derision.

"Then Gaillard added a few facts. And finally, his mother filled out the rest. She said that her son and your husband had spent every weekend of their lives together, even after you and Charles married. Is that true?"

"What has this got to do with poor Serenity? It's ancient history, past and done with. I forgave Charles. He meant too much to me. He meant everything to me. This thing with Don—delayed adolescence, neurotic nonsense." She snorted. "They weren't boys anymore."

"If you set out to find a man who isn't a boy anymore," Dave said, "you're going to be a long time looking. And you haven't forgotten about it. It's not ancient history to you. Don Gaillard's still the enemy. That's why you never mentioned him to me when I asked you to tell me who your husband might run to when he was in trouble."

"They hadn't spoken in years," she said. "That day when

I found them naked in bed together was the last time they ever saw each other."

"They had a place they went to on those weekends, didn't they?" Dave stood up. "And you followed them there. Why? You'd watched them go off together a thousand times."

"To the high Sierras, to the desert, to Baja. Ocean fishing in a hire boat. So they said. Then, one weekend when Chass was busy and Don took the kids, he made a mistake. And Serenity told me all about Uncle Don's little house in the woods, about finding so many of her daddy's things there. What things? Oh, clothes and things." Anna Westover smiled thinly. "Out of the mouths of babes? It was fantastic. All those years I hadn't suspected a thing. And suddenly, at that moment, I knew—I knew and understood it all."

"It was up Yucca Canyon, wasn't it?"

She stared. "Yes. How did you know?"

"And you remembered it when I told you your husband had gone somewhere to hide—when I asked you if you couldn't suggest where that would be. But you kept your mouth shut."

"Because I never in the world would have thought he'd go back there. He promised me." She meant it.

"Doesn't divorce invalidate that kind of promise?" Dave said. "What's the address?"

"Address?" She laughed dryly. "It's wilderness up there. The road's no more than a pair of ruts. I don't think it even has a name. Little box canyon, all overgrown."

Dave stepped to the door. "Can you lead me there?"

She pushed at her hair and laughed helplessly. "You

must be mad. It's been ten years. I don't know how I got there. I simply followed them." Her voice trembled, her eyes swam. "I don't know how I got out. I was blind with outrage and hurt and disappointment and emotions there aren't even any names for." She opened a desk drawer and fumbled tissues out of it to dry her eyes. "No, Mr. Brandstetter—I'm afraid I cannot lead you there." She blew her nose. "It's like a place in a nightmare. Something you wake up from, hoping you'll never sleep again."

"Did they rent it?" Dave asked.

"What?" She blinked, frowning. "Rent it? No. No, they didn't rent it. Didn't I tell you? Don built it. It belonged to Don. He built it so they could have—" But she didn't go on with that. "It belonged to Don," she said again, dully. She shrugged. "Perhaps it still does."

Dave pulled open the door. "Bet on it." The chairs weren't in a circle anymore. They had been pushed against the wall. A game was going on that involved running, squealing, and falling down. Dave said to Anna Westover, "I'll let you know," and walked down the long room, trying not to stumble over children.

"You've hurt yourself." Thelma Gaillard was more noticing than Anna Westover had been. She pushed the screen door and put her head out into the rain to look down the stairs. "You drove here with only one arm?"

"It isn't too hard," Dave said. "There's an automatic shift. May I come in?"

"What's happened?" Looking anxious, she pushed the screen door wider so he could enter. The kitchen was not as tidy as before. Now there were more dirty dishes, not just on the shelf by the sink but on the table. She looked as if she hadn't combed her hair today. She was wearing the same faded jeans and torn sneakers and this time a sweat-top with a hood, dark blue. "Have you found Don?"

"No, but with your help I'm going to."

She shut the door, shut out the cold breath of the rain. "I'm not so sure of that. Don withdrew a lot of money from our savings. Almost all. Twenty thousand dollars." She peered up at him. "Did you know that? Was it to give to Chass?"

Dave nodded. "And Chass promptly lost it. If you were thinking Don used it to travel to some far-off place—he didn't. He's at his cabin in Yucca Canyon."

She had started toward the dim hallway that led to the living room. She turned back. "His cabin? What cabin?"

"How did you happen to learn about the missing money?" Dave asked.

"Well, I phoned the police because you said I should. It was a few days, and then a detective came. He asked a lot of questions. I couldn't tell him much." She smiled wanly. "But you already know that. He said I should check through Don's papers—bills, letters, anything, for clues to where he might have gone or why. Well, I looked but I didn't find anything that meant anything. The detective said check with the bank. At first they wouldn't tell me. Then he went with me." She gave a little unhappy laugh. "I never thought I'd ride in a police car in my life. And they let him see the account record and that's how we found out. But it didn't help find him, did it?"

Dave moved toward the hall. "Where are these papers? In his room?" He found the open door to the room with the neatly made bed. "Is this his room?"

"Yes ..." She said it doubtfully. She stood in the door from the kitchen, fingers pressed against her mouth, eyes alarmed. "But I've been through everything. He's so private, Don is. He hates for people to—"

"I think he's with Westover," Dave said. "And Westover may be a dangerous man to be with right now." He laid his hand on the arm in the sling. "If it keeps him from getting hurt, he won't mind a little invasion of his privacy." The room had only one window, and the rain outside made the light from the window dim. Dave groped for a wall switch and turned on a lamp by the bed. He stepped inside, hearing her footsteps come down the hall, and stop in the bedroom doorway, unwilling to come farther. Don Gaillard didn't give an impression of being able to intimidate anyone, but he had intimidated her. "Closet?" Dave asked. "Chest?"

She jerked her chin. "Bottom drawer."

It was a green-metal fishing-tackle box. She got the key. Dave sat on the edge of the bed, the box on his knees where the lamplight would catch it. He unlocked it, lifted the lid, reached for his reading glasses, and remembered that the lens had popped out and he'd forgotten to ask Cecil to put it back. He squinted and sorted through the papers. None related to the cabinetmaking business: these were personal, insurance, property payments, doctor bills, income tax. There was a membership in a so-called health club that was for homosexuals only, though the paper didn't say so. There was a worn, soiled envelope of snapshots—big, barrel-chested Gaillard, slim little Westover. He tucked them back, frowning.

"You see what I mean?" Thelma Gaillard said.

Dave grunted. Here was an envelope marked in large

type "Joint Consolidated Tax Bill." The flap was loose. He pulled a tax bill from the envelope. It wasn't easy for him to read without the glasses, but he made out the address on the bill. Blurrily. It was for this place, shop and living quarters. He worked the bill back into its envelope and picked up another envelope like it and slid the bill out of that one. He held it under the lamp and narrowed his eyes, trying to focus. His heart bumped. Burro Trail, Yucca Canyon. He laid the bill in the green tin box, closed the lid, turned the key, held the box up to her. "You never knew Don had a cabin that he built himself for weekends?"

"Is that where he's gone?" she said. "I never knew."

Dave stood up. "May I use your phone again, please?" He had to let the receiver dangle on its cord, knocking the wall, while he turned the dial. He caught hold of the receiver and held it to his ear. Not expecting Cecil to answer—it would be hours before Cecil got back from Perez. Dave's own voice answered on tape. He waited for the tone, checking his watch. "Three-forty P.M.," he said. "The address is 29934 Burro Trail, Yucca Canyon. I'm going there now."

Thelma Gaillard watched him hang the receiver in its fork, her face creased with worry. She wrung her hands. "You'll find him now, won't you? You'll find Don?"

"I'll find him." Dave gave her a quick smile and hurried out the door and down the stairs in the solemn rain. He didn't feel solemn. He felt elated.

14

The canyon was hung with rags of sooty cloud this afternoon. The rain fell steady and cold. Anything able to turn green had turned green—oaks, pines, chaparral. The grass among the rocks was thick and high. The potholes in the twisting roads were wider today, deeper, but the Jaguar didn't let him feel them. It took the bends, elbows, the steep lifts and falls of the roads without effort. Even so, his good arm grew tired, his hand on the wheel ached.

He stopped on a plank bridge above the tumbling muddy stream and studied again the map he'd picked up at a shiny bookstore in Santa Monica. He had to squint to make out the map. Burro Trail was no more than a thin scribble maybe a quarter-inch long. It was far back in from the roads he'd prowled along the other morning. He hadn't come within miles of it. There'd been no chance that he'd sight the Rolls, the panel truck, the old Impala.

He laid the map on the empty seat beside him and sat flexing his stiff fingers and frowning to himself. He had passed and left far behind the crossroads with the filling station, general store, building yard. Should he drive back there and ring Salazar? Being alone when he found Westover didn't worry him. Gaillard didn't worry him. But what about the girl? If she was Serenity, how sane was she, how stable? Maybe, after all, she had been the one who tried to kill him.

He gave his head a shake. This wasn't like him. This case was humdrum—attempted fraud on an insurance company. He'd handled a hundred of those in his time, more than a hundred. The car smash and his aches and pains were getting to him. And his goddamn age. And the gruesome background of this one. He saw those shacky blue buildings again out there in the desert, the sandy holes where the girls had been buried. He shivered, though the heating system of the car worked well. He wasn't even wearing his jacket. He wished he knew what Cecil had learned at Perez. Had the Impala come from Jay's dusty lot of high-gloss jalopies? Ah, the hell with it. He was acting like an old woman. He started the car and rumbled it off the loose planks of the bridge and went to find Burro Trail.

It climbed a box canyon as Anna Westover said, two ruts that the new spring grass was doing its best to make invisible. The rainy daylight was dying fast, helped by tall trees, pines and pin oaks. He peered past the batting of the windshield wipers, hoping Westover had switched a light on that would lead him to the cabin. But there was only gloom. He didn't want to show headlamps. He wanted to arrive with as little warning as possible. In the TR this would have been unthinkable. It was noisy. The Jaguar's engine purred like the big cat it was named for, powerful, no need for bluster.

Was what he saw now, back among the trees, the straight

170

line of a roof? He slowed the car, inching it along the bumpy ruts, keeping in his sights that horizontal line until he was sure. He stopped the car, switched off the ignition, set the gears. He stretched awkwardly to paw his jacket off the rear seat, and got out of the car. Under the chill sifting of the rain, he worked his good arm into the jacket sleeve and hiked the left side of the jacket up over his shoulder, over the arm in the sling. He crouched to set the hand-brake, straightened up, and quietly closed the door. He stood for half a minute, gazing up the trail. Had Lovejoy sent that letter? Had Westover picked it up? He sure as hell hoped so. He drew a long breath, expelled the breath, and began to climb the trail.

Even in the growing dark, it wasn't hard to see the marks cars had made coming down out of the woods and going back up into the woods. He followed the marks, slipping sometimes in the mud. The house was farther than he had judged. He encountered the Impala first, facing him, front fender crumpled, dripping rust in the rain, the headlamp smashed. Beyond the Impala stood the rain-glossed Rolls. And beyond that, half in some kind of ditch, tilted, Gaillard's panel truck. The light was bad, the paint faded, as Thelma Gaillard had said, but he could make out the yellow lettering, as much of it as showed above the dripping brush: "llard" and, below that "fted furniture." He didn't know why it put him in mind of an abandoned hearse.

The cabin looked deserted. It wasn't. Sounds told him that—the slap of a screen door, the drum of heels on a porch. A rifle went off. The slamming noise it made echoed in the rainy hills. A bullet whined past his ear. Someone shouted, "Hold it right there, mister." Dave stepped behind a tree trunk. The voice called, "You're on private property. You're trespassing. Get off."

"Charles Westover?" Dave called. Could it be Westover? It sounded like a boy's voice. The rifle slammed again, the bullet hit the tree trunk, and knocked loose bark that fell on Dave. He brushed it out of his hair. He shouted, "I'm from Banner Insurance." The rifle went off again. But the bullet didn't sing, and it didn't strike anything. He thought it had been fired into the air, and he couldn't make sense of that. He shouted, "We wrote you a letter. About your claim. Did you get the letter?" The gun went off again. The bullet hit the tree high up. A pinecone rattled down through wet branches and hit the ground with a splash. Dave shouted, "I need your signature on some forms. So we can pay you." Why was he saying these things? Why didn't he just turn around and leave? He turned around to leave, but someone was in his way, someone scrawny. The blond girl, in her raveled sweater, dirty jeans, and dark glasses. The rifle fire had been only cover to let her reach him. A big black machine pistol was in her little hand, and she pushed it into his sore ribs and said, "Not this way, that way. We're going in the house."

"What is Westover so afraid of?" Dave said.

"You think about being afraid," she said. "Don't worry about him. Move. Move." She jabbed him with the gun barrel and pushed him. He wished she sounded nervous. She sounded confident, even bored. He walked ahead of her, watching his step on the rough and muddy ground in the dying light. As if his falling or not falling were a matter of importance. He grinned sourly to himself.

"You're Serenity," he said, "aren't you?"

"That doesn't mean it's over," she said. "It's only just beginning. Climb the steps."

"Why aren't you with Azrael?" he said.

She laughed and poked the gun hard into his lower back, right against the spine. "Climb," she said.

He climbed. The stairs were well made. Paint had worn off them but the planks were thick and sturdy, meant to last. He thought about Gaillard, hanging onto this place in the frail hope of getting Westover back here some sweet impossible day. Only it hadn't been impossible, had it? It had just been all wrong. At the top of the stairs, Dave lifted his eyes. The rifleman was scrawny too. He held the rifle under his arm, pointed at Dave. The roof overhang made the porch dark, so there was no way to see his features. He looked as blond-haired as Serenity. And his eyes were so pale they seemed to glow.

He backed through the cabin door, keeping the rifle barrel leveled at Dave. The girl pushed Dave ahead of her across the porch and through the door into a room that was pitch-dark. The door closed. A match was struck, and the flame showed Dave a second man, slight, gray-haired, bending above a kerosene lamp on a table of thick, polished planks. The man touched the flame of the match to the wick of the lamp and the wick took fire softly. The man blew out the match and set a slim, smoky glass chimney over the flame. The top part of the man's right ear was missing. He looked at Dave sadly and slumped down on a spooled maple sofa with faded chintz cushions. He looked thoroughly beaten.

"Are you Lovejoy?" he said.

"I work for him," Dave said. "I'm Brandstetter."

"That's good," the rifleman said. "That means we've got a name to contact at the insurance company. That's very good. Where did you leave your car? Is there anyone in it? You came alone?" His pale eyes were crazy and he smiled. It was a wide smile meaning nothing. He had cut off his holy-man hair and beard. But there was no mistaking him.

"You're Azrael," Dave said.

"Azrael died in the desert on the way to Las Vegas," Azrael said. He sat down at the other end of the sofa, the rifle laid carelessly across his knees. But Dave wasn't going to escape. He could feel the girl's breath on the back of his neck. "His soul is in limbo, waiting to be reborn in a far country, to begin a new life."

"You had Serenity follow you to Nevada," Dave said. "You dumped the van out there in that barranca and doubled back here." He looked at Westover. "It wasn't your idea to apply for her insurance. It was theirs. They wanted the money to escape on."

Westover sighed and nodded glumly.

"You didn't leave your house to avoid creditors," Dave said. "These two brought you here." He glanced over his shoulder at Serenity. "You remembered this place. Uncle Don's cabin in the woods. A good place to hide until the insurance company paid up."

"Too many neighbors down there," she said.

"Where is Gaillard?" Dave said.

Westover made a sound and put his hands over his face.

"You want to see Gaillard?" Dave had thought Azrael's smile was wide before. It stretched wider now. He looked straight into Dave's eyes. The effect was like an electric shock, but less pleasant. Dave tensed to keep from shiver-

174

ing. Azrael jumped up off the couch, laid the rifle on the table, scratched a match on its blue cardboard box, and tilted the chimney of a lantern to set its wick afire. He picked up the lantern by its wire-loop handle. "Come with me." He went down the room, making a sound that might have been a chuckle. It resembled the noise hyenas make around a kill. Serenity's gun nudged Dave and he moved after Azrael.

Dave asked Westover, "Why don't you run away?"

Westover's mouth twisted. "Because if I try, he'll kill Serenity. Oh, he will. Oh, yes. And you, too."

"Move," Serenity said. And Dave moved, through a door Azrael had opened and down a short hallway, half-open doors on either hand, and through a kitchen strewn with empty cans and wrappers and stinking of garbage. The lantern swung in Azrael's hand. At a door that led outside, he turned back to give Dave another look from those insane pale eyes and to make the hyena noise again. He was amused. He pushed out a screen door and the lantern stairstepped downward. Here were more of Gaillard's sturdy steps. They ended in a puddle. The rain fell through the swinging nimbus of the lantern up ahead, sparkling. Dave stumbled on clods and rocks. Brush lashed his trousers, soaking them, chilling his legs. Branches slapped his face. He wiped the wet off his face with his hand. The land sloped off. Azrael had moved faster than they. The lantern stood on the ground and Azrael moved in its glow. For a second, Dave couldn't figure out what he was doing. Then he knew. He had a spade, and he was digging. Dave stopped.

"I don't want to see this," he said.

"You said you wanted to," Serenity said. "Anyway, it doesn't matter what you want. All that matters is what he wants. That's all that matters in this world. You'll learn that. You'll be happy when you learn that." She jabbed him with the gun. "Go on. Go on down there."

Dave shut his eyes. Thelma Gaillard was looking up at him, pleading, wringing her hands. *You'll find him now, won't you? You'll find Don?* He opened his eyes and went on down to where Azrael was throwing heavy clods of mud to one side and making the hyena sound. He grinned at Dave.

"You wanted to see Gaillard?"

He threw the spade aside and dropped to his knees and dug with his hands, scrabbled with his hands like some animal after some other animal in a burrow. The glow of the lantern in the falling rain made it stranger even than it was. In Dave's mind, Cecil said, This is weird. Azrael made a new sound. A long-drawn growl of satisfaction. He turned his sharp small-boy face up to Dave, his mad eyes. With animal quickness his hand caught Dave's and yanked Dave to his knees in the mud. Azrael grabbed the lantern and held it low over the hole he had dug. A face looked up at Dave, a face already eaten at by the things that live in the ground, waiting for such faces, but a face Dave knew, the face of Don Gaillard. A terrible smell rose out of the hole. Dave turned away and vomited.

"You wanted to see him," Azrael said. There was no expression in his voice. He got to his feet, set the lantern down, picked up the spade, and began filling up the hole again. "I wanted you to see him. I want you to believe in me." The wet earth slopped into the hole. "I want you to remember my deeds. By their fruits shall ye know them, all right? I always mean what I say. Mortals say"—he was panting a little with the effort it took to move the sodden earth—"I'll kill you. But they don't mean it. When the angel Azrael says I'll kill you he means it."

Behind and above where Dave hung on hands and knees, trying to make his stomach stop convulsing, Serenity laughed. The spade slapped the wet earth. Dave felt splashes of mud from the grave. The spade rattled when Azrael tossed it aside again. Dave felt arms under his arms. He was lifted to his feet. He couldn't look at them in the lantern light. He kept his face averted as they climbed back to the cabin. In the main room, Charles Westover sat slumped on the couch just as they'd left him. He lifted his beaten eyes to Dave.

"They made me eat his heart," he said.

"He wanted to help you," Dave said. "He loved you."

Westover nodded. "I know." But it didn't appear to matter to him anymore. "He drove into the yard. I saw him from that window. Smiling. He looked so happy." Tears were supposed to break in here. Westover waited for them, or seemed to, but they didn't come. He looked bitterly at Azrael. "He shot him. Over and over again. He didn't even have time to get out of his truck." He looked at Dave again. "You were lucky."

"Is that what you call it?" Dave said.

"Perverts," Azrael said. "Perverts."

"I was glad my son was gone," Westover said. "When they came, I felt like thanking God that Lyle was gone. Is he all right? He didn't kill himself, did he? He said he was going to kill himself. It wasn't true, was it?"

"It wasn't true," Dave said. "He's all right."

Azrael said to Dave, "Sit down. You don't look very well. I don't want you to get sick: I've been waiting for you. I have plans for you. If you carry them out, I won't kill you. I won't even kill the pervert, here. If you don't carry them out, I'll kill him." He sat opposite Dave at the table with the lamp on it. "And if you try to bring anybody else here, I'll kill them too."

Dave felt sick about the message he'd left for Cecil.

Azrael got up, went out of the circle of lamplight, came back dragging a wooden box the size of a milk crate. He shoved it with his foot to the edge of the circular braided rug that was under the table. The lamplight fell on it. With a muddy shoe, Azrael lifted the loose lid. "Ammo," he said. "Between us, Serenity and me—we can kill five hundred people before they kill us." His eyes fixed Dave again. "We can, and we will. Remember that."

"What are these plans of yours?" Dave said.

"You are going to telephone Mr. Lovejoy"—the scrawny boy sat down again—"at Banner Insurance Company, and tell him that you are in the hands of the Angel Azrael."

"I didn't see any phone lines leading up here."

"Serenity will drive you down to the crossroads, and you'll use the pay phone in the booth outside the filling station. You won't try to run away or yell for help. You will deliver the message and come straight back to the car and straight back here. Because I'll be timing you. And if you're late, I'll kill Mr. Westover, the same as I killed Mr. Gaillard. I will put him in the same grave, and the two perverts can rot into each other and be one flesh forever and ever, amen."

Westover gave a soft moan from the couch.

"What's the message I give Lovejoy?" Dave said.

"That the Angel Azrael will kill you and bury you in a muddy hole unless Banner Insurance Company pays him one hundred thousand dollars. In cash. New, unmarked bills. At three o'clock tomorrow afternoon. You will pick up the money yourself. From Mr. Lovejoy himself. He will bring it to the beach—Cormorant Cliffs. Nobody ever goes there. He will come alone. After he has put the money in your hands, he will go back where he came from. And you will bring the money here to me. If you don't, if you are even the least little bit late, I will kill Mr. Westover. If you do, if you come back on time, alone, I won't do anything to him. I won't do anything to you."

"And Serenity?" Dave said.

"Serenity will go away with me forever," Azrael said.

Serenity crooned, "In a great silver bird in the sky." Then she said sharply, "Wait." She ran to the front window. Curtains were drawn across it. She stood with her back against the wall and with a finger made a gap between the edge of the curtain and the window frame. There was the slight rattle of venetian blinds. Azrael had the rifle again. He was standing, pointing the rifle at the door. "Someone's out there in the trees," Serenity said.

Azrael glared at Dave. "Who did you tell?" He didn't wait for an answer. He ran to the other front window, stood beside it as Serenity stood beside hers, edged the curtain away, squinted out into the dark and rain. "I don't see anything. Blow out the lamp."

"I heard a car stop in the road," Serenity said. "I saw somebody move in the trees."

Dave stood. He told Westover, "Go into the kitchen."

Westover simply stared at him. He didn't move.

Azrael said, "Shut your mouth." He gestured with the rifle barrel. "Blow out that fucking lamp."

The lamp was all glass. A lot of kerosene was in the well. Dave picked up the lamp. Steps thumped on the porch. Cecil's voice called, "Dave?" Dave yelled at Westover, "Run!" and Westover's eyes opened wide and he jerked alive. He ran for the hall. The venetian blinds clattered. Serenity had got the machine pistol caught in them. "Dave?" Cecil called outside in the rain. Azrael lunged for the door. "Cecil, hit the deck!" Dave shouted. Azrael tore open the door. With a knee, Dave tipped the table on its side. He slammed the burning lamp down hard into the crate of bullets and threw himself behind the tabletop. The light of the kerosene flared up and made the room bright. Azrael's rifle went off. Then the bullets in the crate began to go off. Crazily. In every direction. Serenity screamed. Crouched behind the table, Dave felt the thick wood jar and jump from the force of the bullets. "Ah!" Azrael said. "Dave?" Cecil said. Something was wrong with his voice. A river of flame shot across the floor. Bullets shredded the curtains, shattered the frail blinds, the window glass. The couch began to burn, the ragged curtains above the couch. The bullets banged and ricocheted. Empty casings tinkled like rain, spent lead rattled down. There was smoke, and a strong smell of gunpowder.

"Westover!" Dave shouted. "Run for help."

If there was an answer, he didn't hear it. He crouched behind the tabletop. Bullets kept slamming into it. He felt them strike, heard the wood splinter. Smoke swirled. He got smoke in his lungs, convulsed with coughing. When he got over that, he glanced behind him. Azrael and Serenity lay sprawled in front of the open door, the boy across the girl, both facedown. Blood had puddled around them. It shone bright red in the firelight. Dave blinked against the smoke, trying to see out the door. Fire climbed the walls. By its light he made out the soles of long shoes at the edge of the porch in line with the door. As if Cecil had been struck just at the top of the steps and had fallen backward down the steps. Ah, Christ.

The explosions of the bullets stopped. But the rafters were burning now, crackling, spitting down a rain of sparks. And it was hot, too hot for him to stay here any longer. He started to straighten up, and more bullets exploded and he crouched again. He crawled, keeping flat as he could, the side of his face rubbing the floor. His head struck the softness of the children's bodies. Their blood wetted his face. He tried to push them ahead of him out the door, but they were heavy and he couldn't get purchase. He lay coughing, bullets whining over him, expecting at any second one of them to drill into him. Then a rafter fell. He didn't see it. It was behind him. But he heard its roar and felt the jar of its weight through the floor under him.

He lunged over the bodies, struck the porch and rolled, screaming at the pain in his shoulder. He scrambled into the shelter of the cabin wall beside the door and hunched there, coughing, panting. His clothes were sweaty, and in the sudden cold he shivered. The bullets stopped exploding. He waited. There might still be more. There didn't seem to be more. Now there was only the crackle and roar of the flames inside the cabin. He crept on knees and one hand and, flinching in the fire heat, dragged Azrael onto the porch and across the porch. Westover stood below the porch, staring.

"Take him down into the trees," Dave said.

Serenity's hair, jeans, and sweater were burning when he dragged her out. He beat out the small flames with his hand. He dragged her to the porch edge. Westover came for her and carried her away. His feet went out from under him and he sat down in the mud, the girl in her scorched and smoking clothes lying across him. He struggled from under her. Even over the noise of the fire, Dave could hear him sob. Somehow, he staggered to his feet with the girl in his arms and bore her away into the rainy darkness. Dave dropped from the porch to the ground. He swayed for a second with the pain in his shoulder. He saw the shadowy Westover lay the girl down and kneel beside her. Dave knelt beside Cecil. The boy was covered with blood. Dave laid fingers on his neck, under the hinge of his jaw. Flames were licking out the front windows of the cabin. He dragged Cecil away from the cabin, then ran skidding down to Westover. Westover looked up at him, face wet from more than just the rain.

"She's dead," he said. He stretched out beside her in the mud, put his arms around her, and laid his head on her breast. "No no," he said, "no no."

Back of them, the cabin roof fell in. It gave a hoarse roar. Sparks and flame reached up into the rain, lighting the tall pines and pin oaks with a nightmare orange glow. Dave stepped around Westover and his dead girl and crouched by Azrael. There was no need to feel for a pulse in this boy's neck. A red ragged hole as big as a fist had opened in his forehead. His strange pale eyes looked straight up into the rain that fell upon them. Dave reached across and shook Westover's shoulder. Westover raised his head. His eyes were open, but he wasn't seeing.

"I'm sorry," Dave said, "but I've burned my one good hand. I don't think I can drive." He climbed to his feet and, hurting the blistered hand, dug into the pocket of his ruined jacket for his keys. He held them out to Westover, who blinked at them for a few seconds as if he didn't know what they were, then wiped his runny nose on his sleeve, took the keys, and got up off the ground. Dave said, "One phone call ought to get fire, paramedics, ambulance, the works."

Westover's face twisted. "But she's dead," he said. "They're both dead."

"Not the black boy," Dave said. "The one who came to the door. He's alive. And I'd like for him to stay that way. My car is the Jaguar, a little way down the road. Can you hurry, please?"

Westover looked at the keys in his hand. He looked at Dave. Something cleared in his eyes. He nodded, and began to run, slipping in the mud, stumbling over roots, down through the trees and the dark rain toward the road.